The Long
Way Home

The Long Way Home

Andrena Sawyer

TATE PUBLISHING
AND ENTERPRISES, LLC

Published by Tate Publishing & Enterprises, LLC
127 E. Trade Center Terrace | Mustang, Oklahoma 73064 USA
1.888.361.9473 | www.tatepublishing.com

Tate Publishing is committed to excellence in the publishing industry. The company reflects the philosophy established by the founders, based on Psalm 68:11,
"The Lord gave the word and great was the company of those who published it."

Book design copyright © 2014 by Tate Publishing, LLC. All rights reserved.

Published in the United States of America

ISBN: 978-1-68028-538-3
1. Fiction/ Christian/ Romance
2. Fiction/ African American /Christian
14.10.20

Special thanks:

To every reader, church, bookstore and book club that chose to read this book and to share it with others.

Mom, dad, Ethleen and Hannah: thank you for your endless support and encouragement. Hannah, your pen will change lives.

Afa, Philip, Marcus, Lutisha, Waheedah, Alyssa, and all of my dear friends who are really much more like family: I am appreciative of your support, encouragement and prayers.

To every woman that's looking for a reason to believe: your story is not over! The breath you just took is evidence of that. Be encouraged (1 Peter 5:10).

Prologue

"Well, if you can't respect that, then maybe it's best that we go our separate ways," Alonna said confidently. Although she tried her best to sound assertive, she wasn't so sure she believed the words herself. This was the third guy in two months that she'd had to turn down, but she was determined to keep her promise to herself. As she looked down at her promise ring, she recalled the day all the youth from her church participated in the ceremony, and they, too, promised their parents they would keep themselves pure until the day they married. Over the years, many of them failed to keep that promise. Some had kept their transgressions a secret, but for others, the evidence was their inflated bellies and guilty faces. Not so for Alonna. When she made that commitment, she'd meant it.

After some encouragement by her mother, she'd walked down the aisle as a symbolic showing of her decision to wed Jesus Christ. Not once had she regretted her decision. Sure, she had been called uptight and a prude several times by the boys in her class, and many of the other girls did not want to hang out with her because she was never quite cool enough, but none of that mattered to her. She was more committed than ever to keep that promise.

As she moved her gaze her from the ring to Charles, she wondered how things could have gone so wrong. She had invited the co-captain of the football team over for a study date, but it was obvious he had more in mind than just studying.

As she looked at the 250lb linebacker sitting on her small twin bed, it seemed that it was sure to end up being another lonely Friday night. She knew his reputation, but she was naïve enough to have him over on a night which her roommate would be out of town. Perhaps she could have been the one girl to make him change his womanizing ways. She quickly found out how wrong she was. Within minutes of entering the room, he was reaching for the buttons on her blouse. She'd tried to swipe his hand away several times, but Charles was a professional at getting what he wanted. Perhaps the rumors were true that he could have any girl he wanted, and he chose a different "girl of the week" throughout the school year. Regardless of whether the rumors were true or not, she now knew better than to become his next victim.

"Charles, I mean it. This is not what I am about." She repeated herself as she struggled to pull her clothes back together.

"What are you talking about?"

Charles Johnson looked perplexed. No one had ever spoken to him like that before. Alonna knew that, and she could tell from his eyes that it made him more determined to achieve his goal.

"It's time for you to leave." Alonna walked to the door and held it open.

"If you don't agree with what I'm saying, then you need to leave."

She was more determined than ever before.

"Why do you have to be so uptight?" Charles asked.

"You're not the first, nor will you be the last to call me uptight, Charles," she responded sarcastically, stretching her hand into the empty hallway.

"Baby, no one ever has to know."

"I am not your baby."

Alonna had heard those words before. It seemed every guy since the tenth grade made their own promises about keeping secrets and being the first. She was not interested in either, and since she had never been good at keeping secrets, she fled from those guys as fast as she could. When she saw that Charles was determined not to listen, she walked to her bed, gathered his belongings and threw them out in the hall.

"I need you to leave now. If you don't, I will call Nicole and you will have to explain why you are an unwanted male in an all-female dormitory." Her voice was getting louder. She was proud of herself. She'd dodged another bullet, and she was determined to dodge as many more as necessary to keep the most important promise she'd ever made.

"You're not that cute anyway. I was bored, and that's the only reason I even came here."

"Well, you reached out to me, and not the other way around. Please leave."

Alonna tried her best to maintain the sternness in her voice, and hoped that he did not notice that his words had stung.

"Whatever. Let me know when you're ready to grow up."

With that Charles walked out. Alonna walked to her refrigerator and took out a carton of Haagen Dazs ice cream. Tonight was sure to be another lonely night. That was fine by her; at least she had her principles to keep her company. For as long as she could help it, she would prove all the naysayers wrong and keep that promise she made to herself, even if it was the last thing that she did.

Chapter 1

All I really wanted was some of your time. Instead you told me lies when someone else was on your mind.

Alonna turned up the volume on the radio. She'd purposefully set the dial to her favorite Arlington station because a clear signal would alert her that she'd crossed city lines. As the voice of Whitney Houston rang through the speakers, Alonna shifted back in her seat. The twelve-hour journey was almost over, and she would soon be back with the people she missed the most. Her derriere, as her mother would say, was sore beyond comprehension, but thoughts of her best friends kept her alert, awake and stepping a little too hard on the gas pedal. In the six years that she'd been gone, this distance was the most unbearable part.

Now I see, that you've been doin' wrong. Played me all along and made a fool of me baby. You got it all wrong to think that I wouldn't find out. That you were cheatin' on me baby. How could you do it to me mmm babe?

The lyrics to *Heartbreak Hotel* seemed to perfectly summarize her stay in Chicago. When she made the announcement that she was moving back home, there were those who accused her of running away. She'd argued that she was not running away from anything, but rather

10

running toward something—home. To her, home was not just a location, but it was where she'd left the only people who seemed to ever really care about her.

Along with her two best friends, Nicole and Arianna, she'd missed her sister and mother the most. Unlike most young girls, Alonna's relationship with her mother grew strong during her tumultuous teenage years, and their bond remained intact well through her young adult years. Her relationship with her father, on the other hand, had been strained for as long as she could remember. As the oldest child, Alonna often had to play the role of father as she and her younger sister watched him fight a vicious battle with alcohol.

At 15, when she started her first job at a local restaurant, she would divide her meager paycheck in halves; one of which would go to her mother to help with household items and bills, the other would be spent purchasing things for her and her sister that their mother could not afford as the sole provider for the family.

She remembered the day she returned home from cheerleading practice to find her mother curled up on the living room couch, under a pile of tissues. Delores Jones had tried desperately to wipe her face and flash her dazzling smile, but Alonna knew that something was wrong. Despite her mother's protests, her father later told her and her sister that the doctor found what they thought was a tumor in her mother's chest. For a moment, her world shattered. They later found that the tumor was not cancerous, but that event taught Alonna never to take her mother for granted again. The bond they now shared was nearly unbreakable.

In addition to the strong relationship she had with her mother, she also had a strong relationship with her only sister, Grace. Although Grace was twelve years her junior, Alonna always fought to protect her closeness with her. Grace was often called her mini-me, not only because of their striking resemblance, but also because of her feisty and gregarious personality.

"I'm going to be something great. You'll see." She remembered the day the hopeful teenager said those words after being rejected from the school drama club. Alonna had no doubt that Grace was talented, and despite the odds being against them with an alcoholic father, something about her sister's confidence made her believe too.

The very thought of seeing Grace and her mother again brought a smile to Alonna's face. However, even they would have to wait a few days for her visit. First up on her itinerary was a trip to see Ari and Nicole—her two best friends for the past ten years. Although not blood related, the three had forged a sisterhood that started their freshman year at Howard University.

She turned the radio up louder as she thought back to their first meeting during freshman orientation week. There were times that their friendship still puzzled her because the three could not have been more different. Ari was the grounded southern belle from Atlanta, Georgia, while Nicole was the sassy girl from Southern California with some roots stemming from across the Atlantic in Nigeria. Alonna fit in perfectly with the two as the tough girl from Baltimore whose wit was both impressive and intimidating for those who did not know her.

Alonna was initially drawn to Ari out of curiosity. In contrast to Alonna's caramel skin and long curly hair, Ari had smooth cocoa skin, and a closely cropped and stylish haircut. Many often commented that she looked like she belonged in the latest issue of *Ebony* or *Essence*

Magazine. Alonna had observed the quirky teenager while moving into her dormitory on Freshman Move-in Day. She had large wide-brimmed glasses, and her hair was styled in a short but chic hairstyle. Alonna had watched as she patiently held the door for many families who were also busy moving their daughters into the dormitory. She greeted each parent with a warm hello followed by a polite "sir" or "ma'am." Not only did her slight country twang betray her, but Alonna thought her level of courtesy indicated she must not be from the area. The two later bonded in the school cafeteria over their fondness for buffalo chicken pizza and all things red.

With Nicole however, things were a bit different. Nicole was born to a Nigerian-American mother and a Mexican father, making her one of the most eclectic people to walk across Howard University's campus. Her smooth creamy skin, light brown eyes and long straight hair added to her celebrity-like good looks that made her the envy of many of the girls on campus. Alonna had also met her during the first week of school during their dormitory meeting when she learned that Nicole would be her Resident Assistant.

The three friends had found that despite their differences, their commitment to their faith was the initial anchor in their relationship. While in school, they fought fiercely to protect their innocence and to continue in the ways that they had been taught were right.

Alonna could remember that through another health scare from her mother, and despite her father's verbal abuse, it was Ari and Nicole that were there. Their prayers and support strengthened the foundation of their relationship. During the six years she spent in Chicago, one of the most difficult things was being away from Nicole and Ari, who both chose to remain in the DC area after graduating. Knowing she would be close to them again helped her make the decision to move back to Virginia.

The familiar smell of the remaining cherry blossoms floating in the air reminded her of the spring break trips she took with the two during college. Alonna opened the sun visor in the car to make sure that nothing got in her eyes. She could hardly contain her excitement that she would be seeing everyone in a short while.

Alonna felt the vibration of her cell phone. Without looking at the screen, she knew instantly who it was.

"This is the fourth time you've called me in the last hour. I will be there soon," She laughed.

"Well, excuse me for checking on you," Nicole teased.

"Thank you. I will call you when I am a few minutes away," she said as she hung up the phone.

"Just a few more minutes," she said excitedly to no one in particular.

She had taken the twelve-hour journey by herself, and with only two stops to fill up on gas, she was right on schedule to be at Nicole's house before 3pm.

Despite her mother's protests not to drive late, Alonna enjoyed driving through the night because there was very little traffic and the quiet of the road allowed her to think. Something she found hard to do over the last two years. Now, the sun was back up and her adrenaline was pumping. The thought of being able to hug her friends and family motivated her for the last few minutes of the trip.

Alonna pulled the top of her red convertible up as she pulled into Nicole's driveway. She caught a glimpse of her reflection in the rearview mirror. Her loose curls now looked frazzled, and her lipstick had dried out. Her caramel complexion was highlighted by the freckles that she'd inherited from her mother, and her hazel eyes, inherited from her father, were said to be her most alluring feature. She'd never been one to pay too much attention to her looks, but she'd always been told that she possessed a natural beauty. She usually wore her dark shoulder length hair loosely, but Alonna decided to pull her hair into a ponytail. Although she was only going to her best friend's house, it was better that she look halfway decent knowing that Nicole and Ari probably had a few surprises up their sleeves.

As Alonna walked up to the front door, she noticed that the pictures did not do Nicole's new home any justice. Nicole always had the most elegant taste of the three, but she had outdone herself this time. At thirty years old, as a top account executive for one of the most respected engineering firms in the area, Alonna knew Nicole was making enough money to purchase such a luxurious house. There were some who had accused her of using her looks and assets to climb up the corporate ladder, but Alonna knew that Nicole had the brains and foresight to compete with anyone. For her to be able to plan and purchase her home while many of their peers were still paying credit card and tuition debts was no surprise to those closest to her.

As she walked up the steps and rang the doorbell next to the heavy oak door, Alonna admired the beautiful garden on the front lawn. She noticed someone look through the front curtains, and seconds later the two best friends were hugging as if the reunion would be the last time they would see each other.

Nicole stepped back and took a look at Alonna.

"What in the heaven?" she squealed.

15

Alonna laughed, "I've missed you too Nik. I couldn't tell you how close I was because I wanted to surprise you."

Nicole reached for Alonna's bags.

"If I'm doing the math currently, you should not be getting here for another two hours."

"There was no traffic on the road," Alonna replied as she walked into the living room.

"Some things never change." Nicole shook her head referring to Alonna's lead foot.

"I'm just glad you made it here safely. You look amazing!" Nicole exclaimed.

Alonna glanced over her friend one more time. How she managed to keep her figure and stay a size 6 defied Alonna's logic.

"You look very good too, Nik."

"You know me. I try." Nicole joked as she did a playful catwalk the length of the living room.

Alonna was mesmerized by how well decorated the room was.

"Follow me. I have a surprise for you." Alonna heard Nicole say before she could comment on her friend's beautiful home.

Alonna smiled a knowing smile, thankful that she'd applied another coat of lipstick. She knew her friend very well.

"Girl, come on" Nicole responded.

Alonna happily obliged. She knew that there was no way that her friends would not try to make her return as elaborate as possible.

As Alonna stepped into the kitchen, on cue everyone in the room screamed in unison "surprise!"

Alonna stopped just short of the kitchen entrance. She looked around the room, and spotted Ari, along with must have been thirty different people gathered around the kitchen island. Alonna was thankful again for the two minutes she took to reapply her lipstick and fix her hair before coming in. She was also thankful that she had not stopped at Steve's Sub Shop to buy the sundae she had been craving her entire trip back. Judging from the amount of food and desserts on the counter, that stop would have been a waste of her time and money, and it would not have put her any closer to her goal of losing twenty pounds. She made a mental note to resume her diet the following day. For today, she would indulge and enjoy the long overdue reunion.

Alonna looked over at Nicole and then Ari and shook her head in between laughs. She truly did have the best friends in the world. She wondered how Ari managed to keep it a secret, because of the three she was the only who could be counted on to reveal a secret.

As if reading her mind, Ari said, "don't worry, Nik didn't tell me the details until three days ago."

Everyone laughed, including Alonna, as she basked in the joy of reuniting with the two people that were closer to her than even some blood relatives. Finally, she felt safe. People here did not know about the struggles she'd encountered in Chicago, and no one could make judgments about the poor choices she'd made. She found the greatest comfort, however, in knowing that no one, not even Nicole and Ari, knew about the decision she'd made that sealed her fate and made her return home.

"I didn't even see any cars in the driveway," She said as she went around hugging each guest at the party.

"That's why they call her the master planner," someone added from the back.

She glanced over, but could not see who was talking behind the wall of people with expectant smiles waiting for her to make her way over to them.

Alonna joined the laughter of the rest of the group. She could not have imagined a better homecoming celebration.

Chapter 2

I am definitely not twenty-one anymore.
Alonna groaned and looked over at the alarm clock. It was already noon, and she was still in bed. Delores Jones would have a fit if she could see her, but between her twelve-hour trip and surprise welcome back party, she'd earned the right to sleep in today.

She'd forgotten how wild and entertaining her old friends could be. For hours, they reminisced about old professors, their antics during college, and celebrated each other's successes in recent years. By the time Alonna knew it, it was well past midnight. Ordinarily, that would not have been an issue for the self-proclaimed night-owl, except that the fatigue of her trip had settled in, and now she was experiencing aches that were more fitting for someone her grandmother's age.

Although she was grateful that Nicole had allowed her to use her guestroom for as long as she needed, Alonna had set aside time today to begin her apartment search right after working on her business plan. She loved her best friend, but she knew that finding a place of her own was of top priority if their relationship was to remain intact. Her time in Chicago had spoiled her in that regard. There, she was able to rent a luxurious condo at a fraction of the price they would rent for in Virginia. In the last month she'd done some online searches and found three condos similar to where she lived in Chicago. If she could finally get out of the bed, she would go to tour at least one of them today.

Alonna rolled over to the sound of her cell phone ringing. Seeing her sister's name on the caller ID brought a smile to her face. In so many ways Grace reminded Alonna of herself. At age sixteen, all Grace had to do on Saturday mornings was help around their parent's house with a few chores. Since it was just the three of them that meant there was very little to be done. Alonna remembered that when she was growing up the list of chores for cleaning up after five people, including a cousin who lived with them, was never-ending. The bathrooms never seemed to stay clean, the dishes to be washed were endless, and it seemed like she was constantly helping her mother pick up after Grace who was a rambunctious toddler at that time. Alonna smiled and reached for the phone. She had to admit that despite her numerous protests back then, she missed those days. She especially missed Grace.

"Hello, snookums," Alonna said groggily, referring to Grace by the nickname that she'd given her when their mother brought Grace home from the hospital. Despite Grace's protests that she was too old, and that Alonna embarrassed her by calling her that, the nickname was something that Alonna valued because it reminded her of Grace's innocence and her own simplicity back in those days.

Grace exaggerated a sigh, expressing her displeasure. Alonna smiled, knowing that deep down Grace valued the nickname as well.

"Morning, Loni," Grace said referring to Alonna by the nickname their entire family called her.

"What's up, and why do you insist on calling me at unholy hours during the weekend?"

"Because you so-called adults need to learn some responsibility. It's noon, and the world is passing you by."

Grace laughed out loud at her own joke.

Alonna had to admit, the girl had a decent sense of humor.

"Yea, yea, yea," Alonna responded. "What do you need? Money, or an advocate?"

Grace laughed. "Actually, neither."

Alonna was pleasantly surprised. "Really? So you called your big sister just to shoot the breeze?"

"What does that even mean?"

Alonna laughed, sitting up on her bed. "Sorry, I forgot the generation gap."

"Whatever, Loni," said Grace, oblivious to Alonna's reference.

"So, I lied. I wanted to know if I can borrow fifty dollars to put toward a dress I want to buy for a school dance."

"Grace, why is it that you don't have a j-o-b?" Alonna asked, before going on a rant about how she had her first job and more responsibilities at the same age.

"Alonna, please don't start. All I need is fifty dollars," Grace pleaded.

"If all you need is fifty dollars, I bet a j-o-b would solve that problem."

"Alonna, please. I know. I'm going to get a job, but right now, I just need your help."

"What kind of dress is this anyway?" Alonna asked.

She knew that Grace was a reserved girl, and was probably not going to wear the short and skimpy dresses that many teenagers tried to wear. Their parents would never allow her to parade the streets, as they called it, in something unfitting anyway, but she still wanted to know.

"Loni, you're becoming more like momma everyday!" Grace exclaimed.

Alonna cringed hearing those words, partly because she knew they were true. She'd began to notice the patterns in herself.

"If you must know, it's similar to the dress that Ledell wore to the Grammys."

Alonna was unsure of who Ledell was, but assumed that it was whoever the latest teen sensation was at the moment.

"Alonna, all I need is fifty more dollars, and the dance is next week. Momma said she would take me to the mall this evening if I had the money."

While Alonna selfishly enjoyed seeing that her younger sister still depended on her for some things, she had a soft spot and did not want her to feel she had to beg her for anything. She had done enough of that when she had to beg her father for things, only to be rejected, as a young girl.

"Fine, Grace. I'll deposit the money in your savings account, but I want to see a picture of the dress before you buy it."

Alonna teased her sister some more and made a mental note to deposit some money in her account a little later. She would check her account to make sure she had enough to surprise her with a little more than she asked for.

"Thanks, Loni." Alonna could feel Grace's smile over the phone.

The two talked for a few more minutes about Grace's plans for the dance, as Grace revealed that although she did not have a date, she and her girlfriends were going to go together and enjoy each other's company. Alonna smiled. She was proud of the young lady that her baby sister was becoming, and silently hoped that she would stay on the straight and narrow, something she was not able to do.

When Alonna hung up the phone, she no longer felt sleepy. She looked down at her freshly painted fuchsia-painted toenails, and willed her feet to move. With no other option but to tackle her long to-do list for the day, Alonna got out of bed, took a shower and slipped on her favorite jogging suit. Her closest friend in Chicago, Amy, had brought it for her when the two became workout partners. By the end of that first summer, not only had Alonna gained a slimmer figure by losing fifteen pounds, but she gained a friendship that sustained her through her most trying times in Chicago.

An hour later, Alonna got in the car to head to her favorite café for breakfast and to finalize her business plans for The Journey House. As she drove she thought about how not much seemed to have changed about her hometown. Alonna drove with the convertible top down to capture the movement, sounds, and smell of the sunny Saturday. She ignored the persistent urge to stop in many of the clothing boutiques that lined the main avenue that ran through downtown Arlington. Maybe she, Nicole and Ari could do some window shopping after their dinner date later in the day.

She looked in the rearview mirror at her backseat that was still piled with small items that she needed to store in Nicole's garage until she found her own apartment. She smiled confidently, knowing that to some of the people she left in Chicago her move back home was crazy, especially because she was finally building a comfortable and independent life for herself. At twenty-eight, she had a luxurious condo, and she'd finally started to have a good group of dependable friends. Most importantly, however, was that she'd finally gotten over the breakup with Ray, at least enough to go on several dead-end dates prior to her big move. None of that mattered to Alonna. She had taken a step of faith and was not looking back.

She remembered when she called her mother to tell her that she decided to move back to Virginia. She was not surprised. She laughed as she began to notice that none of those closest to her were surprised. This was quite the contrast from coworkers and associates in Chicago who questioned her decision-making skills as she opted to resign from her coveted position as Director of Youth Development.

Compared to what she was hoping to gain, nothing else mattered; not the job, her comfortable two-bedroom condo, or the budding social prestige she was beginning to gain. Alonna had her own plans in mind.

****

When she finally arrived at the café, Alonna was relieved to see that it was just as she had left it. The café was frequented by local students from surrounding universities. While many of the students were away for summer break, it seemed that the café was still full of customers as it was also a favorite among local residents. Alonna grabbed a cup of her favorite iced beverage and a Danish and set to work on her business plans.

When she was considering her move back home, Alonna purposed that it would be an opportune time to pursue her lifelong goal of building a youth center for kids across the bridge in the rough parts of Southeast Washington, DC. When she was in college, Alonna felt helpless and unequipped to act on her desire to give back to

24

the kids she often saw on the streets and local neighborhoods. The idea of The Journey House came to her during her sophomore year. Despite the twists and turns in her life, the idea never left her. It was only until recently that Alonna decided to pick things up again to make her vision a reality.

She had spent over ten years of her life devoted to community development, but dealing with the bureaucracy of other's organizations. Enticed by the idea of working for herself, Alonna began a business plan to build a center that would provide mentoring, tutoring and other much needed services to local teens and their parents. Part of her new plan included getting up early during the week and working on Saturdays, even when she did not feel like it.

She looked down at her watch, it was already 2:30pm. Her dinner date with Nicole and Ari was not until 8pm, so she decided that she would work until 4:30, deposit the money for Grace, then look at one of the four apartments today. Motivated by the thought of hanging out with her girls, Alonna let the sounds of the busy café lull her into a zone as she started writing the ideas that had been keeping her up at night.

Chapter 3

Despite her numerous attempts at falling asleep, Alonna was still having a difficult time. She'd tried counting sheep, reading a book, and even turning the radio to a classical music station, but nothing seemed to be working.

Earlier that Saturday, she had enjoyed the reunion celebration with Nicole and Ari. The three started the night at their favorite Thai restaurant. Nicole and Ari had continued to frequent the restaurant so much so that the waitress immediately directed the three outside to their favorite table when she saw them coming. As always, the conversation was good, as the three caught up on stories of love lost and found, jobs, family, and various other life events. Although she'd heard the story numerous times, Alonna listened as Nicole talked about her promotion to Director of Marketing at MARZ—a local engineering company.

Growing up in Baltimore, Alonna knew that MARZ was notorious for discriminatory hiring policies. In junior high school, Alonna remembered her parents discussing the company being sued by a middle-aged African American man who had been passed over for several promotions and then terminated without reason. The man had alleged discrimination, but lost the case. However, it was enough to mar the image of the company amongst many minorities in the area. At age thirty, Nicole had to have made some kind of history, and Alonna could not be more proud.

For Ari, the biggest story of the night was her relationship with Kyle. Of the three, Ari was the only one in a relationship. However, Alonna questioned how healthy the relationship was. During their sophomore year, Ari developed a crush on Kyle that lasted until the beginning of their senior year. Alonna could remember the endless nights she and Nicole would have to stay up with her to do damage control to her self-esteem after she saw Kyle with other women. Her obsession with marriage never helped. She made it very clear from day one at school that she hoped to find her husband, be married by age twenty-five, and have her first child by age twenty-eight. Now, at age twenty-nine and no ring in sight, she was finally coming to terms with the fact that things were not working out the way she'd imagined.

Tonight's conversation, like many others before, revolved about Kyle's reluctance to marry her. Alonna thought it was selfish that Kyle did not appear to be any closer to marriage than he did on their first date, but she kept her thoughts to herself. As usual, she and Nicole listened attentively and offered advice when appropriate.

Amidst the great food and even better conversation, the highlight of the night, for Alonna, came as the three were discussing their next stop for the night, which would be a new reggae lounge in the heart of DC on U Street. They had Nicole's Nigerian heritage to thank for their exposure to African and Caribbean music.

As they waited for the waitress to return with their check, Alonna heard her name across the busy restaurant, and immediately recognized the voice of Mike, her favorite cousin. She loved and adored Mike, who was extremely protective and most times behaved like the older brother she never had. Growing up, the two were inseparable especially because his father took care of her mother when Alonna's father failed to do so. When she struggled to pay her tuition at school, it was Mike's father who had stepped in to pay the portion that her mother could not afford. In fact, she sometimes considered her uncle more of a father figure than her own. Although born to the same mother, her beloved grandma Emma, the two men could not have been more different.

As he walked toward them, Alonna could noticed that Mike was not by himself. As they got even closer, Alonna recognized one of the three people with him as her childhood friend, Mali. She jumped up with excitement toward her cousin as he picked her up in a loving embrace. Undaunted by the looks of other patrons in the restaurant, the groups exchanged hugs and pleasantries, as Mike and his friends managed to grab chairs from an empty table nearby.

"You look great girl," Alonna remarked to Mali once they were all seated again.

"Thank you. So do you," Mali responded.

"I'm trying to keep up with you," Alonna Joked. "How do you do it?"

"This is what having twins will do to you," Mali laughed out loud.

As Alonna and Mali spoke, she was happy to hear that things had been going well for her. Their relationship had been strained during their sophomore year after Mali learned that she was pregnant. Alonna remembered being surprised because Mali was brought up in a strict religious home. When the two were growing up, Mali's mother often cautioned both of them against distractions, and charged them to do their best in school, and to keep away from neighborhood boys that wanted their "stuff." When she first heard the news, Alonna remembered how much she judged Mali, none of which were ever spoken directly to her, of course.

As they talked, she quickly remembered her own transgressions, and was immediately flooded by the guilt of her own hypocrisy. She wondered if there would come a time when she would feel another emotion, other than guilt, at the memories. As she had often opted to do, she disregarded the overwhelming feeling, and reported highlights from her life in the past six years. She confessed failures and obstacles that were safe to mention, like her failed engagement, which she always blamed on her previous fiancé, or her dislike of her previous home in Chicago. The two had been talking for nearly thirty minutes when a deep voice startled her.

"Are you going to eat that?"

"As a matter of fact, I am."

How rude.

Alonna answered without looking up at the person who would have the audacity to ask her such a question.

She could hear Mali snickering. When she noticed that the looming shadow was not leaving, Alonna looked up and was surprised to see the tall white man standing over her. She recognized him as one of the men who came over with Mike.

"What are you 6'5?" She asked sassily.

"Actually, 6'2" He responded in an even tone with a smirk on his face.

"Well, whatever you are, you are too big to be standing over women like that."

Alonna narrowed her eyes. She could feel her neck moving the way it did whenever she wanted to give someone a piece of her mind.

She looked up at the stranger intensely. He had piercing blue eyes. She wondered what his man's connection was to her cousin, and why he felt comfortable enough to interrupt her conversation and ask for her food.

"I was just kidding," he chuckled.

"Do you mind if I sit here? Mali has been hogging up all your time." He said pointing to the chair next to Alonna.

"Someone is obviously sitting there," she rolled her eyes at him and directed her gaze back at Mali.

Mali chuckled as she got up. "Girl, don't mind him. I have to freshen up anyway. Now that I have your number, we can set up something and hang out sometime."

Alonna smiled politely. She was looking forward to talking some more with Mali, and she silently chastised her for creating the opportunity for the rude stranger to sit beside her. She looked up at Ari and Nicole, who also seemed engrossed in their conversations. She looked over at Mike who was leaning a little too close to Nicole. Some things never change, she thought to herself. Alonna let out a disappointed sigh as she realized that they may not be going to the lounge anymore after all. Alonna signaled for the waitress and decided that she might as well have dessert if the plans were changing.

"So, can I sit here?"

"Whatever. It's a free country," was all she could think to say when she suddenly remembered that he was still standing beside her.

"My, aren't you the friendly type?" he remarked sarcastically as he pulled up the chair across the table.

His sense of humor was a bit dry, but at least he was not rude, Alonna noticed. She decided that as long as he remained that way, she could tolerate him.

"Are you a close friend of Mike's?" she asked.

"We went to school together."

Alonna flashed her famous "fake smile" as Nicole called it.

"I'm Shawn," he struck out his hand.

His grip was firm, and Alonna could not help but feel like his eyes were piercing into hers. They were a deep blue, with specks of grey around them. His dirty blonde hair was cut close to his head, and when he spoke, Alonna noticed that his teeth seemed an almost unnatural shade of white. He reminded her a bit of the movie actor, Channing Tatum. He was definitely what most would consider handsome—those who were into that type.

"Alonna, Mike's cousin." She responded, looking through the menu.

"Nice to meet you, Alonna."

Alonna nodded her head.

"We were supposed to be going to the night club down the street, and Mike saw you sitting down and made us come in here." Shawn volunteered as if Alonna had inquired.

Alonna flashed another one of her smiles. It was only a matter of time before this guy got on her nerves so bad that she could no longer be polite.

"I'm glad he did now." Shawn continued.

"So, I noticed the P4YD bracelet."

"Yea, it's hard to miss the neon orange," she said sarcastically.

Shawn laughed. "I know. I used to work with Professionals for Youth Development when I lived in Uganda."

He rolled up his sleeves to flash his own neon green bracelet. As he rolled up the sleeves on his dark blue dress

31

shirt, Alonna could not help but catch a glimpse of his bulging bicep. She had to stop herself from looking any further, because the more her eyes roamed, the more she noticed what a nice physique he had. He was definitely an athlete of some kind.

"When did you live in Uganda?" She asked to be polite.

"I lived there for three years when I worked there as an English teacher."

"Really? I've always wanted to go to Uganda. I worked with P4YD in Chicago."

With that, the conversation took off. It was one hour later before Alonna heard Mike calling out that he was going to leave whether or not Shawn was ready. Alonna scowled at him. It wasn't enough that he had ruined her plans for the evening, now he was interrupting one of the best conversations she'd had with anyone in a long time.

In the hour that they talked, she'd observed that not only was Shawn well-read and had a decent sense of humor, but his charming personality was a perfect compliment to his handsome features. Alonna pretended as if she wasn't threatened, but she could not help but notice that several women in the restaurant locked their gaze on him, hoping to catch his glimpse. All night, the way he talked to her was as if she was the only person in the busy restaurant. Had she not sworn off men or dating, she might have been intrigued enough to flirt back with Mr. Shawn Williams.

****

Alonna let out a frustrated sigh. Even recapping her day was not enough to fix her insomnia. Some nights were restless nights, and Alonna struggled to sleep. Despite having an eventful day and weekend, tonight was shaping up to be one of those nights. On nights like this, the weight of the guilt rested heavily on her shoulders as she thought back to the incident.

She questioned when the compromise started. Surely it had not all happened overnight, but it seemed to her that overnight everything changed. One day she was in a church crying her heart out to the God she called both father and friend, and the next day she was sitting in her bathroom floor begging for forgiveness for the wretched act she was about to commit. God help her the day that anyone finds out, that she, the same one who was vocal and shook her head in disgust at the idea, had been to the very same place that many of peers had gone to—peers that she'd turned her nose up at. She thought she was different, but that one day and that one decision forever changed her life. That day, she learned she was not so different. She was just like everyone else—living a lie. While her mind and body told her that it was time to move on, the guilt of her past would not allow her to simply move on. She'd been through so much. She'd managed to close one chapter of her life that, even on her worst day, she hoped she never had to return to.

As she did on many nights, she curled up in bed and wept, crying herself to sleep.

Chapter 4

Thankful that the week had gone by quickly, Alonna put the last of her bags in the trunk. She had been so busy that she barely had enough time to pack for her trip. She woke up early and spent much of the morning loading up her car with things that could be stored at her parent's home while she continued her apartment search. The two hour drive to Richmond was just what the doctor prescribed after a long two weeks of catching up with old friends, working on The Journey House and apartment hunting.

Within minutes she was heading south of Highway 395. Thankful that there was very little traffic for a Saturday morning, the sound of her ringtone coming from the car's speakers pulled her out of her thoughts. After nearly getting into a car accident while texting one day, Alonna had decided that the investment to get a Bluetooth set-up was well worth it. She looked down at the dashboard as the phone rang again. She did not recognize the number of the incoming call, but reluctantly answered the call as the choir's smooth sounds on the radio faded away.

"Hello?" Alonna asked, more out of irritation than courtesy.

"Well, hello there."

Instantly Alonna recognized the voice, and was surprised by the smiling etching its way onto her face.

"How did you get my number, Shawn?"

"It's amazing what buying your cousin a round of drinks can get me."

Alonna could hear him laughing. She had not noticed the night before how infectious his laughter was. That irritated her more.

"So, you bribed my cousin to get my number? I'm assuming that whatever you have to say to me must be very important."

"Actually, yes, and if he wasn't the designated driver last night, I might have brought him another round to get your address so I can talk to you in person."

Alonna let out a laugh.

"Good intentions or not, if you showed up at my house uninvited, there is no guarantee you wouldn't have been arrested for trespassing."

Shawn must have enjoyed the playful exchange between the two of them, because Alonna could hear him laughing heartily on the phone.

"So, seriously, how may I help you?"

"Well, I was calling to see if you are free tonight, because I'd like to take you out, without both of our entourages."

"That's awfully kind of you to ask, but I'm actually going out of town for the rest of the weekend, and I'll be back next week."

Although she was technically coming back on Monday, Alonna did not want to get his hopes up. She was intrigued by him, but not enough to disregard her promise to herself. The thought of another heartache sent her into an emotional whirlwind.

As Shawn probed about her trip, Alonna continued to give illusive answers. One thing was for sure, he was determined and undaunted by her snide or short responses.

35

She had gotten the vibe that he was interested in her that night, and now he was confirming it. Alonna finally gave up and determined that there was probably no harm in having just one conversation with him.

Ninety minutes later, she was in her parent's neighborhood. She was still very unfamiliar with the new neighborhood, and it was only when she heard the GPS indicate she was at her destination that she realized how far she'd driven, and how long she and Shawn had been talking. Before she could unbuckle her seat belt, she saw Grace darting through the front door.

"Were you waiting by the window or something?"

Alonna laughed as she got out to embrace her sister. She stepped back to look at Grace who now appeared to be at least four inches taller than her.

"Don't say anything about how tall I'm getting," Grace said as if reading her thoughts.

Alonna laughed, "Well, you are tall. I mean, you're even taller than me now."

"Alonna, you are only 5'3. Everyone is taller than you." Grace gave her a playful shove as she walked around to the other side of the car to get her sister's bags.

"Didn't your mother teach you not to put your hands on your elders?" Alonna called after her.

The sight of the blinking light on her seat reminded Alonna that Shawn was still on the phone. She ran back to the car, half-expecting that he had hung up by now.

"I am so sorry." She said as she picked up the phone.

"No worries." She could hear him smiling.

"I figured you were home and got distracted."

"Distracted. That's a nice word for rude, I guess." She laughed.

36

"No worries."

He was smiling again.

"I didn't realize we had been talking for so long."

"Me either." Alonna responded.

"I guess that's a good thing."

There was a short pause.

"Listen, I'll let you settle in, and I'll call you later tonight."

Alonna was unsure about whether the last part was a question or a statement.

"Thanks, I'll talk to you soon."

For Alonna, soon meant anywhere from tonight to next year. She had the feeling that for Shawn, soon meant as soon as possible.

She hung up the phone and walked back over to her sister.

"Who was that, Loni?" Grace teased.

Alonna narrowed her eyes and jokingly pushed Grace away as she grabbed a few things from the car. As she walked closer to the front door, she could smell the aroma of macaroni and cheese, baked barbecue chicken, sweet potatoes, and her mother's famous homemade caramel cheesecake. The perpetual diet that she was always on would have to wait for the next two days.

"Hello," Alonna said to no one in particular as she walked through the door.

Her mother, with the grace that she always possessed, walked out of the kitchen wiping her hands on her apron.

"Hi, baby."

Alonna reached for her mom's embrace. The familiar smell of home-cooked meals, mixed with her mother's favorite Elizabeth Taylor fragrance filled her nostrils. Her mom's hugs had gotten her through many rough times, from high school heartbreaks, financial woes and even broken relationships. She took a step back to get a good look at her mother. There were noticeably more grey hairs on her mother's head, and more wrinkles on her face, but Delores Jones had not lost her beauty.

Alonna could remember looking through pictures of her mother in high school. She was tall and thin, with the same caramel complexion and freckles that Alonna had. Her hair always seemed perfectly coifed, and even in the pictures, her smile seemed to light up a room. Her mother was known by most as a quiet but god-fearing woman. Alonna often wondered if that was the reason she stayed in a seemingly loveless marriage for over thirty years.

"Ma, how are you? It smells so good in here!" Alonna exclaimed.

"I'm fine, baby." Her mother smiled as she hurriedly walked back to the kitchen.

"I cooked all your favorites, but we have to wait about an hour or so for your daddy before we can eat."

Alonna rolled her eyes. She wanted to spend her two days at home with minimal arguments, so she held her tongue. Her mom was an expert at that skill, and Alonna had learned that from her as well. She admired her mother's devotion, but sometimes felt sorry at how someone so kind could also be so weak.

"Alright, ma," was all she could say.

"Grace and I will just unload and put my things in the garage then."

"Wait, I didn't sign up for that." Grace called out from the kitchen.

"I'll give you ten dollars."

No sooner did Alonna say that, Grace was standing by the door with her hand extended. "After you," she said jokingly.

Alonna gave her mother a knowing smile as she and Grace walked out to the car.

Nearly two hours later, Alonna heard her dad's car pull into the driveway. Her dad had the same car for over twenty years and while he called it a classic, Alonna and Grace often joked about how classic must be a code word for jalopy. However, she was too hungry to joke today. All she could do was focus on the aroma still coming from the kitchen, and not on how her father was once again depriving the family without regard for anyone else.

In the two hours that Alonna had been there, she was unaware of any phone calls or attempt to let the family know that he was running even later than expected. Alonna walked to the kitchen, and noticed Delores busying herself setting the table. Despite her insistence, Delores equally insisted that Alonna was home to rest and would do no such thing. As tired as she was, she could not bring herself to argue with her mother about it.

Minutes later, Alonna heard the front door open. Unlike his wife, Willie Jones was never a sentimental man, and not even the sight of the daughter he had not seen in several months was enough to cause him to be so.

"Hey, Loni," she heard him call out from the living room.

Not that Alonna expected it, but as Alonna poked her head out of the kitchen, there was no reach for a hug and no emotion. His deep baritone voice carried through her parent's modest home. Even from the distance of the kitchen door, Alonna could see the signs of aging on her father as well. His hair had been salt and pepper colored for some time, but Alonna noticed that there was now much more grey than black.

Willie Jones was a proud man, and it seemed his chest was permanently stuck in an upheld position. Also unlike her mother who was a proud devoted Christian, Willie Jones professed to be a Christian, but Alonna had seen little evidence of such. He went to church only on holidays like Christmas and Easter, and often spoke badly about the so-called hypocrites. Growing up, Alonna had been dumbfounded by the irony of one person calling another a hypocrite, when he did the same thing he accused others of doing.

Alonna walked over to him, "hi, daddy."

Even if he did not want to hug her, she would initiate it this time. As Alonna reached over to embrace her father, she expected the usual stench of rum, vodka, or whatever the hard liquor of the day was. Instead, she took in only the scent of old spice. Instantly she was back in her childhood. Back then, she could sit on his lap for hours as he played games with her and told her stories about his childhood in Mississippi. She wondered what happened to the smells had seemed permanently etched onto his clothes.

"Can we eat now?" Grace called out from the kitchen, interrupting the awkward embrace between the two.

"You don't have to tell me twice." Alonna walked toward the kitchen.

She'd missed her mother's cooking, and had been looking forward to this meal for some time.

Chapter 5

The time with her family went by quickly. The meals had been delicious, and the conversations with her mother and Grace had done her heart well. With the exception of the phone calls from Shawn, she'd spent most of the weekend completely devoted to her family. She'd treated Grace to a mini-shopping spree on Sunday, after the two of them and their mother spent the afternoon getting manicures and pedicures. While she still could not have a meaningful or lengthy conversation with him, she'd even spent a little time with her father on Monday morning.

As she loaded the car with the rest of her belongings, she could see the sadness in Delores and Grace's eyes. Good-byes had never been easy for them, especially when she lived far away in Chicago.

"I only live two hours away now, ma."

She returned her mother's tight squeeze.

She turned her attention to Grace.

"Take care of momma, and make sure you listen to everything she says. You're not too old for a spanking," she teased her sister.

"You stop that," Willie Jones added is he put the last bag in the trunk.

"You know your sister has never given us any trouble."

Alonna hugged each of them individually and waved good-bye as she walked back to her car.

Minutes later, she was back on the highway toward Nicole's house. As she drove through highway 395, she wondered to herself why she stayed away for so long. The entire weekend was great, despite her tumultuous relationship with her father. Although she wished things were better, she gave up on that relationship after her junior year in college.

She remembered the phone call she received from her father, two months into her freshman year. Alonna could remember only two times she had known her father to cry. Once when his mother died, and the second she did not see, but could hear when he called to tell her that he and her mother were getting a divorce. For a man who had been unfaithful and treated her mother like a doormat for years, she'd wondered why he would cry that she'd finally gotten enough strength to leave him, or at least threaten to do so.

Hours later, Alonna pulled into Nicole's driveway. She had been so preoccupied with her own thoughts that she had no idea how much time had passed by. It was before 5pm which meant that she would have the entire house to herself, something she had not had since being in Virginia.

Alonna first unloaded the bags of food that her mother packed for her. She chuckled to herself because the running joke in her family was Alonna's inability to cook a decent meal. Just as she did when Alonna was in college, her mother had heaped a lot of food in containers that she hoped would last Alonna until her next visit. As the visits spread farther and farther apart, the more food her mother would send her away with. Alonna took the containers and headed for the door with Nicole's spare key. Within minutes she had the food packed away in the freezer, and was ready to take a quick nap before Nicole arrived home from work.

Chapter 6

"How is it that you get the hookup to everything?" Alonna heard Ari exclaim from the kitchen.

"Just call me Nicole the deal-maker," she heard Nicole say as she walked into the living room with a turkey sandwich and potato chips.

"What happened?"

"Well, your friend over here just got us tickets to the hottest place in town!" Ari exclaimed.

Alonna was not sure how she did it, but Nicole had managed to score VIP tickets to the grand opening of the new Jazz lounge opening in downtown DC. She was quickly learning how well connected Nicole had become while she was away.

"You can sit here and wonder all day," Nicole said as she started up the stairs, sandwich in hand, "or you can go get ready because the show starts in an hour and I will not be late on your account."

Ari narrowed her eyes. "She knows I can't get home in time to make the opening."

"You two are about the same size anyway, get something from her closet."

Before Alonna could finish her sentence, Ari had already made her way upstairs to Nicole's room.

An hour later the three sat in the seats that had been reserved just for them.

"I'm really trying not to be upset with Kyle about this whole marriage thing, but the more I talk, the less he seems to get it." Alonna and Nicole listened as Ari talked about the latest incident between her and Kyle.

"What do you mean?" Alonna asked.

"Well I can't think of any other creative ways to hint to Kyle that I want to get married."

"Is he saying that he does not want to marry you?" asked Nicole.

"Not exactly," Ari responded.

"Last night we were at his aunt's house, and I overheard her ask him why his grandparents don't know about me if he is serious about me."

"Wait a minute. I thought you already met the whole family. What's the holdup?"

"Girl, you and I are both confused. I am having some serious doubts about this whole relationship now."

"Wait a minute, Ari," said Nicole, "you and Kyle have a great relationship. Don't start doubting everything because of this little spat."

"It's not a little thing. We have been together for six years, and I still don't have a ring on my finger." exclaimed Ari flashing her bare finger in Nicole's face.

"Calm down," Alonna cautioned.

She really wanted to caution Ari against rushing to get a ring, especially if Kyle's character was questionable. To start that conversation, however, would require that she get into the sordid details of her failed engagement, and she was not in the mood to do so.

"Loni, I can't calm down. I have been with Kyle for too long now, and I was under the impression that we were both moving toward marriage. I was obviously wrong," Ari

45

said, now on the verge of tears.

Alonna moved closer to comfort her friend.

"Now look, Ari, just because he has not introduced you to his whole family does not mean that he does not want to marry you."

"Don't you guys see," explained Ari, "Kyle and I have been together for over six years. We all know how close he is to his family. If I was a priority to him, he would have told everyone about me by now."

Nicole nodded her head in agreement, "I know sweetie, but there has to be an explanation for this. I always thought that his grandparents knew about you. In fact, I thought you said you guys were planning a trip to South Carolina to see them soon."

"That's what hurts the most," replied Ari, "He always told me that they did, and I never had reason to question it."

"I understand honey," stated Nicole, "well, let's calm down about this, I'm sure there is a good explanation."

Alonna, always the optimist, listened to Nicole, but deep down inside she feared the deeper implications of what she was hearing.

"So, what's new with you guys?" Ari asked. She hurried to change the subject, but Alonna could see the anxiety in her eyes.

"All is ok over here." Nicole said. "Remember Tom in accounting?"

How could they not remember? Nicole had been giving them a play by play of his antics after alleging that the director of the company was using reverse discrimination tactics to employ only women and minorities. Each time Nicole told the story the three had a good at laugh the allegations. Before Nicole could go any further, the lights dimmed as the featured group was introduced.

Chapter 7

Are you really going to do this?

Alonna had asked herself that question several times over the past hour. Every time she decided against doing it, she thought about the alternative, which was to spend another Friday evening alone. She rushed to get the matching black sweater hanging in the closet.

She could hear all of Nicole's questions from the room upstairs. Despite the fact that she was hesitant about going out tonight, she could not allow Nicole to continue the interrogation any further. After three weeks of turning him down, Alonna had finally given in to Shawn's request for a simple dinner, as he called it. She hoped that she would not regret her decision. She was relieved that only ten minutes into the evening, and he was already passing all of the tests, including the interrogation session going on downstairs.

Instead of waiting outside and blaring the car horn like one of her previous dates, he'd walked to the door and waited for her in the living room. From what Alonna could hear, he seemed to be making it through the grilling session with Nicole and Ari. She had dreaded the meeting between him and her friends due to their continuous reference to the movie *Jungle Fever*. Despite Alonna's insistence that Shawn was just a friend and that the two were just going out "for dinner," Nicole insisted that Shawn bring her back home safely and not try "anything funny on the date." The fact that he could laugh off Nicole's sometimes off-putting comments, meant that he had passed the second test.

When they walked to the car, Shawn opened the door for her. Alonna made a mental note to relay that he had passed test number three.

As they entered the restaurant, Alonna noticed that their waitress, a petite blond, was very attractive. She paid close attention to how much attention Shawn was paying to her, but was relieved to see that she had his undivided attention. With the exception of looking up to order his food and to say thank you, he barely even looked at the cute blond. The idea seemed silly, even to her, but she'd started using this as test four because of Ray's notorious wandering eyes.

Alonna could remember the embarrassment of being out on a date with him while he gawked at other women right in front of her. She smiled to herself as she thought about the ridiculousness of making Shawn take a test that he had no idea he was taking.

Early on in the evening, they made polite conversation. She asked about his background and listened as Shawn explained that although he graduated with his Master's degree two years ago, he could not find work in his field. After nearly two years of waiting, he finally found a job as a mechanic doing what he enjoyed most. As it turns out, he and Mike worked at the same shop, and that's how they became close friends. There was something about Shawn Williams that seemed more genuine that most men she'd ever met.

After all of her questions, it was Shawn's turn to ask about her background.

"How'd you end up in Chicago?" He asked as he took another sip of his drink.

"Long story short, it was for work."

Not content with her short answer, Shawn continued probing.

"You seem like a pretty smart woman. Why'd you choose Chicago?"

These types of questions usually irritated her, but they were also usually coming from people trying to pry in her business. Something was different about Shawn though. For some reason he seemed genuinely interested in her story. She looked away from him when she realized he was staring at her waiting for a response.

"There's really not much of a story," she lied

"Like everyone else in school, during my senior year I was desperately looking for a job. After endless nights of filling out job applications and traveling around the country to interview with different companies, I finally received the offer for a lucrative position with one of Chicago's top Community Development agencies. They offered me more money than I'd ever seen before in life."

Shawn looked on eagerly as he listened to every word she said. He wondered if she knew just how beautiful she was. Everything about her was mesmerizing—the way her lips curled when she was trying not to smile, or the way her laugh lit up the room and made him want to laugh along.

When he met her that first night she looked amazing, but it was her personality and wit that he found most alluring. Somehow, she was even more attractive tonight. Her teal dress brought out the green flecks in her hazel eyes, and hugged her in all the right places. The black sweater she wore over the dress confirmed his thought that while she had all the right assets to make any man want her, she was a classy and modest women. Judging by the way she averted her eyes to avoid extended eye contact with him, he doubted that she knew. He'd told himself that he didn't want to be in another relationship after Jessica, but his heart betrayed him every time he thought about Alonna. As he looked at her, he wondered what it would be like to be the man in her life.

Stop that. Right now!

Alonna went on explaining her stay in Chicago. At the time, she was confident that the position was exactly all that she wanted and needed. Her ambition was unmatched. Alonna shook her head as she talked about the grueling years that turned out nothing like she had envisioned. After that second year, when things began to crumble around her, she'd cried herself to sleep many nights, but her determination kept her from leaving. In typical form, she'd set her mind to achieve one thing, and nothing would stand in her way. There seemed to be a supernatural force that beckoned her to stay, despite the fact that year after year, she dug herself in a deeper hole of depression and remorse.

"What made you want to come back? I hear Chicago is a great city for young professionals."

"It is, but I got tired of the city," Alonna lied.

The truth was that in an uncharacteristically impulsive move, two months ago, when the lease ended in her high-rise condo, she'd decided to take the out and move back home. She'd prayed that this move would be better for her than the last one had been.

"I guess I got tired of the city life. I just want to do something now that brings me more fulfillment."

Her eyes seemed to be drifting to a faraway place.

"Like what?" Shawn took another sip of his drink and signaled for the waitress.

Alonna was usually hesitant to tell people about her plans for The Journey House, because she was used to dealing with the corporate types who quickly lost interest in community issues. However, something about the way Shawn listened made her want to tell him.

"How did you come up with the name, The Journey House?"

"I don't know, I guess I just believe that all of us have to go through a journey in life. For some people, the journey seems more difficult. I have always envisioned a place where we can partner with teens who are going through a rough journey and need someone to come alongside them to help out."

Shawn smiled. He admired her transparency, and much like the first night he saw her, he was desperate to learn more about her. Something told him there was more to this story than she was willing to share. If she let him, he'd be willing to wait to hear everything.

Alonna ate another forkful of her dessert. It was her turn to interrogate him again.

"So, what is the status between you and God?" She asked abruptly.

After her relationship with Ray, she'd learned to ask that question early on. She looked up at him and noticed his look of surprise. She repeated her question. His response would determine if there would be a second date for the two.

"Well, me and the guy upstairs are just fine. He does his thing, and I do mine." Shawn pointed to the ceiling, looking amused at his own joke.

"So, are you a Christian, or are you not?"

"Wait, I thought we were going out to dinner." Shawn looked around the restaurant confused. "Did I step foot in a church and no one told me?"

"Sorry, I'm just trying to know you better. Kind of like how you asked me twenty-one questions earlier." She mumbled the last part under her breath.

"Sorry to disappoint you, but religion is not really my thing anymore." Shawn stated after observing the dissatisfied look on her face.

"What does that mean?" She'd heard those words before, especially from Christians who considered their faith more about relationship than organized religion. She hoped that was what he was alluding to.

"I mean, I'm a good person, and I think that should be enough," he said.

"Besides, I try to stay away from the topics of religion and politics whenever I am out just having dinner with beautiful women."

Alonna hoped her discontent was obvious. That was not the answer she was looking for.

"It's no problem at all." Alonna responded evenly as she started picking up her things. With the luck she'd had in relationships, there was no point in continuing this non-date because things would definitely not work out anyway. She should have listened to the tiny voice that first told her that dinner or not, the date was not a good idea. Since she broke up with Ray, her last two dates were with Josh who outright hated God and spent every waking moment trying to convince her of His nonexistence, and Sam who went to church on Sundays but could not have a good time if it did not involve throwing up the next day. Between the two, she'd had enough of men who did not value what she now valued.

"Alonna, wait a minute," Shawn said in desperation.

"Just because I don't go to church like you, that means we can't talk?"

"Talking is fine, but we both know you'd like to do a little more than talking, so let's not waste each other's time because it just won't work out."

Shawn appeared hurt.

"Listen, I'm just going to be completely honest. I don't know what it is about you, but I'm very interested in getting to know you more."

"What can I do to show you? You want me to go to church with you tomorrow or something?" Shawn asked jokingly.

"Actually, that's not a bad idea." Alonna said smiling as she walked away.

She hated to end their non-date so abruptly, but her heart had been hurt enough to last her a lifetime. She had no extra minutes to spare with someone if it was going to be a dead-end.

Shawn picked up his steps behind her.

"Ok, if that's what you want, I'll be there tomorrow."

Alonna turned around and searched his face to see if he was joking.

She gave him the details for the service in the morning and walked toward the door of the restaurant.

"Can I at least pay for dinner and take you back home?"

The non-date had obviously not turned out the way he'd expected.

"Don't worry about me. I'll catch a cab,"

Alonna called out as she stuck her thumb out to hail a taxi. She knew that her actions may have seemed a bit harsh, but she was determined not to waste any more time in anything that could potentially hurt her the way that Ray had.

As she listened to the soulful sounds of Ledelle in the backseat, she could see the driver's moving his head to the upbeat classic. She thought about Shawn Williams. There were several things about him that she enjoyed. However, she'd learned the hard way that a man can be a lot of wonderful things, but if he was not the main thing, nothing else mattered. His virtually nonexistent relationship with God was going to be an issue. There was also the slightly major issue that while he was tall and handsome, he was also white. For that reason alone, they were worlds apart.

She laughed to herself when she thought about what some of their friends would say when she told them she'd dumped a tall, dark and handsome hotshot lawyer, to give a white mechanic a chance.

She hated herself for being so shallow, but she wondered what people would think, especially the people who had known her all of her life—the people who always had grand expectations for her. How could she, after going to one of the best HBCUs in the country, end up with a man like Shawn Williams? All her life, she'd gone against the status quo. However, when it seemed like it most mattered, she struggled within herself. She had a terrible habit of overanalyzing and obsessing about things. Alonna was determined that this was not going to be one of those things.

****

The next morning was beautiful. It seemed, like Alonna, all of the creation was up and alert, excited about Shawn Williams going to church. It had been so long since she was excited about church herself, and now she was inviting others. She knew she'd come a long way. After they left the restaurant the night before, he'd called her to make sure that she got home alright and to confirm that the two would meet at the church the next morning.

Shawn walked slightly behind Alonna. She wondered if the confident, at times cocky, Shawn Williams could actually be feeling unsure of himself. She could not blame him though. If it was her first time setting foot in a church building in years, she would be nervous too. During their phone conversation the night before, she'd learned that not only had he not been to church in years, but he had grown quite cynical of all religion.

With great candor, he'd explained that his father was a well-respected leader in the church who had forced the whole family into Christianity. After years of complete obedience, a church scandal erupted with his father at the center. The church secretary had apparently seen his father and another church member coming out of a hotel. As more allegations came out, his father finally admitted to a three-year affair with another one of the church leaders. The shame was too much for his mother to bear, and they separated and divorced soon after.

Shawn's cynicism was reasonable, because she'd been there, but Alonna knew it would only lead to further questions and frustration. Ultimately, these things left a void that only God could fill anyway.

Alonna slowed her step to be in sync with him, and offered a reassuring smile.

"Don't worry. Everyone I know here is really nice," she whispered.

Alonna had been attending the church since she moved back to the area, and she recently joined the membership class because she felt more at home in the church than every other church she'd ever visited. As they walked up the pavement toward the entrance, several congregants waved hello. Many of the hellos were accompanied by inquiring looks. Having grown up in the church all her life, she was used to it by now. It seemed assumptions were universal in churches. Any time she invited a man to church, or was invited by a man, she got the same looks, no matter which church it was.

She rarely thought about the racial make-up of her church, but today she was thankful that she went to Redemption Nondenominational, one of the most diverse churches in the DC metro area. That meant that Shawn would not stand out as much. After the first month, Alonna had lost count of how many interracial couples there were at the church. Whites with Blacks, Latinos with Asians—no one discriminated—and most people liked it that way.

She looked over at Shawn again, who seemed to be getting more nervous the closer they got to the entrance. She touched his arm to reassure him that all would be ok. As she was trying to reassure him, she said a silent prayer that God would use Pastor Paul to preach a message that would speak right to Shawn's heart.

Chapter 8

"Sometimes, I'm scared you're going to find someone better."

Alonna was startled by his words. It had been six weeks since they went to church together, and they had been nearly inseparable since. He'd enjoyed the service so much, that he voluntarily kept going back. Several times, he even hinted toward an exclusive dating relationship. For her hanging out was fine, as long as there were no titles attached to their relationship. Titles meant expectations, and she was not yet ready for any expectations. Besides, while she was happy that Shawn had agreed to start going to church more regularly, Ray taught her that church attendance had nothing to do with a man's faith.

There were times she felt guilty because she could hear her mother's voice cautioning her about what she would refer to as being unequally yoked. Since living in Chicago, she'd learned that you never judge people by what they said, but by what they did. Ray had taught her that too. On paper he was the perfect guy—a Harvard Law School graduate who was quickly making a name for himself and on the fast track to becoming a partner at his law firm. When she met him, she was most impressed by his supposed love for God. He spoke sincerely about growing up in the church as a pastor's kid, and how he longed to have the type of relationship that his parents had. Since his parents had been married for over 35 years, she, too, wanted to emulate what they had. Three months after meeting him she began to untangle the web of lies that he was so good at weaving. Now she had him to thank for her unreasonable skepticism of all men.

The more she watched Shawn though, the more certain she was of one thing—he was a doer, unlike Ray. Alonna was watching him quietly, and while he was no bible thumper, she was impressed by his integrity and his compassion for other people—all things that Alonna hoped for in a husband. At the thought of marriage, Alonna shook herself out of her daze.

"Huh?" was all Alonna could muster.

His mouth had been moving, but she had not heard a word he said.

"Loni, sometimes I get scared that you'll find someone better than me."

"Whoa there Romeo, let's just slow down a bit," she teased.

She hadn't meant to make light of the moment, because she could tell that he was being serious.

"Besides, if we stop hanging out, who else would I force to take me to Sala Thai every Friday?"

She wasn't quite as good as him when it came to making light of an awkward situation, but she gave him a reassuring smile.

She wondered how someone who was so good looking, and appeared so confident could make such a statement draped in insecurity. At least she was not the only one struggling in that area. She'd often wondered how she would appear if she confessed to the same thing. The reality is that she was often the one who felt like she was not good enough for anyone and that any minute a more beautiful, vibrant, purer woman was going to come and snatch his attention away from her. As much as she did not want to admit it, she was really starting to like Shawn. Having someone call her beautiful several times a day was doing a lot for her self-esteem that had taken a severe beating in recent years.

She looked down at her now size twelve hips that were always sure to remind her of how far she had come. One of the things she had quickly learned about Shawn was that he was as religious about the gym as she was about her newfound faith. Every time the two of them went out, the admiring eyes of both men and women asked what her imagination conjured—how did *she* manage to get with *him*? She wondered how someone like him would be afraid of losing someone like her.

Sure, she was funny and cool. She'd been funny and cool all of her life. In high school she had more guy friends than girlfriends because she was funny and cool. Later she added smart to that list, but only after a few people noticed and were sure to comment on what an articulate black girl she was. For as long as she could remember, she's always had funny, cool, and smart in her bag of tricks—nothing more.

She doubted if funny, cool, and smart were enough to sustain a relationship, because they had not been enough to sustain things with Ray, who she found in bed one day with his twenty-one year old secretary. According to Shawn, funny, cool and smart were at least enough to keep his attention for the moment.

As if reading her mind, Shawn stated, "Alonna, I know we've only been hanging out for a few weeks and

60

you haven't known me that long, but don't you think it's time we went a step further?"

Immediately her defenses went up. She knew it was only a matter of time before sex became an issue. She had made mention, even if it was briefly, that she was celibate. How dare he not respect that?

"Listen," she started as she reached for her purse. "I've already told you, whatever your perverted mind thinks is happening, is not!"

She was furious.

"Wait, what are you talking about?"

Shawn was genuinely confused. He started to reach for her hand across the table, quietly pleading with her to lower her voice because other patron in the restaurant were starting to look over.

"I don't know Shawn, you tell me." She snapped back.

She could hear Ray's voice telling her that her temper was unbecoming and ill-fitting for women.

"You know what, it's ok. I shouldn't have expected anything else." Alonna sat back in the chair. All men really were the same.

"You should know me better by now." Shawn sat back in his chair as well.

"Listen, I don't know what set you off, but I am sure there is some kind of misunderstanding."

Shawn took her silence as permission to continue.

"I am not sure why you assumed what you just assumed, but tonight I wanted to ask you if we could make this thing serious."

He motioned his finger to indicate he was talking about their relationship.

"I know, it's a bit juvenile, but it was a lot cuter and smoother when I was planning it in my head."

It was his attempt at making light of the situation, but Alonna felt his embarrassment, and hers.

It took a few seconds for Alonna to compose herself before speaking. She was embarrassed at having reacted the way she did. She silently chastised herself as once again her insecurities got the worst of her. She reached across the table and gently touched his hand. She secretly loved the way their hands looked together—a mixture of coffee and cream.

"I am sorry for reacting the way that I did."

She did not feel it necessary to explain the root of her skepticism, but he at least deserved an apology. Most days she wasn't quite sure she understood it herself. A gentle move of his fingers indicated his acceptance of her apology.

She looked down as she continued. "Shawn, I really don't see what you are asking me happening."

She left out the part about how she desperately wanted it to happen, but something in her would not allow it. Her heart had betrayed her once, and she could not let that happen again.

"Alonna, you don't understand" he continued. "I've never met anyone like you. I see women every day, and I have not been interested in seeking anyone out since I met you."

She really wanted to ask him why. What made him claim she was special? She chose not to ask for fear of exposing her insecurities even further. Truth was that she needed that affirmation more than anything else at the moment. She fought the urge to accuse him of being a liar.

As much as she looked for evidence, he'd done nothing to warrant that accusation. All she could do was listen.

He leaned in closer. "I know that we have our differences, and I may not be everything you imagined, but all I'm asking is for you to give me a chance."

Alonna smiled to mask the tug-of-war going on inside her. Since returning home, there had been quite a few men that had made similar requests for "a chance" with her. With others, her response was quick and sure. Their motives were clear from the beginning, and she'd learned not to even entertain possibilities that were sure to lead to nowhere.

"Shawn, the timing may not be right." She believed that in her heart.

She noticed the disappointment on his face.

"I like you," she added reassuringly, "but the timing is not right."

She figured she would save him the explanation about the differences in their beliefs, or her concerns that she'd never dated someone outside of her race. All that mattered now was that she was not quite ready for this next step that he was proposing.

"I can respect that," he said sitting up.

Sure, his ego was bruised, but he'd heard her pastor say one time that delay does not mean denial. Shawn smiled.

Alonna was unsure what the smile was for, but she knew Shawn well enough by now to know that this was not the last time that they would have this conversation.

Chapter 9

Thanksgiving seemed to come a lot quicker this year. Maybe it was because Alonna was busier than she'd ever been before. Although she'd found an apartment and was moved in, she was still unpacking and purchasing furniture and other household items. When she was not busy trying to settle in her new home, she was working on her plan for the grand opening of The Journey House.

In the last month she'd applied for a loan, contacted potential investors, and identified the perfect location for the center. As if that was not enough, she signed up to start working with the teen mothers at church. All of her new commitments, in addition to spending all her free time with Shawn, seemed to make time go by much faster. She hadn't realized how busy she was until one evening Nicole commented that Alonna never had time for her and Ari anymore. Alonna had promised that when she returned from her parent's house, the three would be able to resume their weekly dinners to catch up on life.

As had become the tradition since her college years, she arrived at her parent's home the night before Thanksgiving, to find her mother cooking way more food than her family would be able to consume in a day. Alonna knew Delores Jones found pleasure in caring for others this way. The kitchen was her sanctuary, and while she would ask Alonna and Grace to wash dishes and other small tasks, she did not want anyone to ruin the menu she'd literally spent all year creating. The running joke between her and Grace was to countdown to the moment when their mother would start complaining that although she had two capable girls, no one was willing to help her in the kitchen. The routine had become predictable, and to deviate would take the fun out of it.

As she often did when she visited home, she stayed up all night enjoying luxuries like cable television. Tonight, she had Grace were watching a new reality show about teenage girls who underwent plastic surgery. Grace seemed to be enjoying the show, but Alonna was dozing off. She picked up her cell phone on the coffee table and saw that she'd missed a call from Shawn. She looked over at Grace who was still engrossed in the show, and sneaked off to her old bedroom.

"Hello there. I saw a missed call from you," she said when he picked up.

"And you actually called me back?" He asked snidely.

"Yes, smarty pants." She smiled.

Since the incident at the restaurant, they hadn't hung out nearly as much, and she missed him more than she was willing to admit.

"How's it going over there?"

She gave him a rundown of her drive to Richmond, and the way she'd been spending her evening up.

"How's it going for you?"

Shawn explained that he'd decided not to spend Thanksgiving with his family, but rather with friends back in Arlington. The two talked for a few minutes longer before Alonna heard her mother call her from the kitchen.

"I guess I'll see you when you get back." It sounded more like a question than a statement.

"Sure thing."

Alonna hung up the phone. She couldn't quite put her finger on it, but she could hear from his voice that he was up to something.

****

Thanksgiving had been wonderful, as usual. Besides having dinner with the family, her father was barely around, and Alonna liked it that way. The disappointment that used to plague her was no longer there. In fact, she enjoyed not having him around sometimes because it ensured that she could enjoy her time without hearing him argue with everyone in the house, and there would be no snide remarks to her about how she lost a good man because she is too "uppity." As always, her favorite part of the holiday was that Delores had packed enough food that, if portioned carefully, could last her until Christmas.

After retuning early that morning, Alonna had spent most of the afternoon catching up on work that she purposely avoided during her four-day vacation. Just the month before, Pastor Paul had preached a dynamic sermon about being "Good Stewards of Little." He referenced Matthew 25, and explained that as Christians, we are expected to take care of whatever little we were given by God so that He can trust us with more. As he spoke, Alonna had thought about The Journey House. Sometimes, it was difficult to explain her vision to others because other than a business plan, she had nothing else to show for her idea. She knew that the little that she had right now was her

66

vision, and that to be a good steward of it would mean diligence with her talents and time. She needed to be prepared so that when her dreams did come true, she would be able to handle it.

Alonna looked up at the clock. She'd been working for the past three hours, and needed a lunch break. She usually took the time to watch one episode of her favorite television show while she ate as a way to unwind, but today all she needed was some peace and quiet.

She walked to the mailbox, and while she was not looking forward to the pile of bills that awaited her, she needed to stretch her legs anyway. After being officially unemployed for four months, she'd started to exhaust her savings, and bills that she used to pay early, she was now paying late fees on. Most days, this motivated her to work even harder on The Journey House.

As she sorted through the stack of mail, Alonna spotted the green envelope. It had no return address, so she assumed that it was not a bill. Perhaps Nicole or Ari had sent her a cute card, like they used to do when she lived in Chicago. As Alonna opened the envelope, she saw an index card. She smiled at the idea that someone would send her a hand-written note in his day and age. The note read *"Will you be my girlfriend? Please check, Yes or No. Maybe is not an option this time!"* The letter was signed SW. She flipped the card over to find more writing in small print that read *"You are one of the few people who I think would appreciate 'juvenile.'"* Alonna shook her head and laughed out loud.

It had been nearly a month since the dinner incident, and she wasn't sure what she was going to say to him, but she immediately picked up the phone. As the phone rang, she looked outside of her window. Knowing him, his car was probably parked outside of her building waiting for her to respond to the letter. She peeked through the front door of the building; all seemed normal. After the third ring, Alonna heard the familiar voice.

"Well, hello there." His wit was still there, which meant that he was not upset with her.

"Hello there." She smiled.

She knew that he could not see her through the phone, but it seemed the smile was the involuntary, albeit natural reaction.

"Thank you for the note."

"You're welcome."

There was a slight pause on the phone. "So, what's your answer?"

Alonna hadn't thought about her answer. All she knew was that since their spat at the restaurant, she'd missed him terribly. She loved hanging out with Nicole and Ari, but with Shawn, things were different. Maybe it was his sense of humor, or the way he seemed to always look out for her best interest, or maybe it was his openness to accommodate her needs? Whatever it was, she'd missed him.

Ray had taught her several lessons during their relationship. Some lessons she was not proud of, and wished she never had reason to learn in the first place. One of those lessons was how not to follow her instincts. Several times during the beginning of their relationship, she would call him after a fight. He loved it and took advantage of it. Eventually she caught on to how he emotionally manipulated her to massage his ego. She soon learned that although it was her natural inclination to seek peace with him, she had to suppress her feelings to protect herself.

She now found herself doing the same thing all over again—suppressing her feelings.

"Listen, before you tell me your answer, whatever it is, I just want you to know that I really missed hanging out with you this past month."

"I missed you too." Her mouth had betrayed her again, and the words slipped out before she could stop them.

"So, what's your answer? Which one did you check?" He was still smiling.

"Shawn, this is really hard for me."

"Alonna, before you say anything else, I just want you to know that I'm not asking for marriage or anything, I just want you to give us a try. I am committed to making something work between us despite our differences."

Shawn wished that he could explain that he was not interrupting because he was usually rude. In fact, most conversations were dominated by Alonna because he enjoyed listening to her, and could do so for hours. His heart and mind were now betraying him. He could hear Mike laughing at him. Despite the fact that Alonna was his cousin, he would advise Shawn not to "chase after no tail." With Alonna things were different though. He actually enjoyed the chase.

Like Shawn, there were so many thoughts running through her mind. The jokes would never end about how she went to the top HBCU in the nation, and still could not find a good black man.

All she could muster was a quiet "yes."

She smiled as she said it, and she could sense him smiling on the phone too.

"Shawn, I will give this thing a try. I like you, and I enjoy hanging out with you."

Alonna left out the part about her mind prompting her against this, but her heart had betrayed her again, and all she could say was "yes" again.

"I promise that you will not regret this."

She could hear that he was trying to control his voice. Since she met him three months ago, her life had changed. Most days she was convinced it was for the better. His persistence was frighteningly intriguing, and because of that, she could say that after waiting for two years, she was dating someone again.

"I really hope so."

She hadn't meant to respond out loud.

Chapter 10

Alonna reveled in the fact that in such a short time, her and Shawn's relationship was quickly becoming more than she could have thought or imagined. Thursday had become their official date night. No matter how their week had been, or how much work they had to get done, they were committed to spending time with just each other. Sometimes, they stayed in and watched a movie at home, other times they went out to their favorite restaurant, or visited a new hot spot.

Today, Alonna surprised him by coming to his house and cooking his favorite meal: spaghetti and meatballs with a garden side salad, and garlic bread. She served it with his favorite red wine. She loved how simple he was. During her relationship with Ray, she'd learned how simple she was. Although they did not live together, his outrageous demands to have dinner available when he came over after work caused many disagreements between them.

Alonna could still remember the telephone call from her mother one evening after an argument with him. Her mother reported that Ray called her because he was concerned about Alonna's "domestic abilities." Alonna initially laughed because she thought the whole thing was a joke. After a gentle reprimand from her mother, she knew that they were both serious. Ray had wanted a trophy wife who cooked, cleaned, dressed well, and met his physical needs, just like the women on television, but Alonna was far from that. While she did not mind cooking, she did not want a relationship where she was expected to do so every night. She charged that to her generation and her busy schedule. The truth was that although she did not enjoy cooking, she'd made a personal commitment that she, at least, hoped to be able to cook her man's favorite meal. When she found out that Shawn's was spaghetti and meatball, she was elated.

As she put the basket of garlic bread on the table, Alonna noticed Shawn smiling at her. It was obvious he wanted more than just the meal that was being put on the table. From what Alonna understood, he'd had a difficult day at work, and she'd asked him to sit down and not lift a finger.

After noticing the hunger in his eyes, she walked around his chair and put her arms around him. "What? Why are you smiling at me?" She playfully nibbled at his ear.

Shawn looked up at her and kissed her on the forehead.

"Just thinking about how lucky I am," he said.

"That you are, Mr. Williams," she responded, trying her best to hide the fact that she was now also getting excited.

Most times they were together, she tried her best to control herself, but it seemed almost impossible. She loved his cologne, and the way his hands enveloped hers when they held hands. His broad shoulders seemed the perfect resting place whenever she felt burdened or insecure. There were times when she found the excitement trickling and her thoughts wandering about the day when they could become one, in every sense of the word. Alonna shook her head to snap her thoughts back to a safe and chaste place. She could hear Nicole's voice, *"girl, you betta get a hold of yourself right now! When your body starts telling you to do things that your Spirit says no to, it's time to split!"*

He took her arms gently and guided her to the seat next to him. The air was thick with their desires. As she sat down, he pulled her closer to him. As their lips met, Alonna could feel the tension in his body ease. She let his hands wander. He'd never tried to cross her boundaries, and now, although her mind was telling her no, after over two years of celibacy, her body wanted it too. She felt his hands go down her back and underneath her shirt. She held him tighter and basked in the warmth of his mouth and body. Shawn was becoming more ravenous, and so was she. He panted heavily, and as he unbuttoned her shirt, she could feel his mouth traveling down her neck. They were no longer sitting, but rather lying on his kitchen table. She had manage to take off his shirt, and started in on unbuckling his belt.

As much as she'd tried to drown it out, she could no longer ignore the cries of a baby in her head. The sound had become so familiar, and although she knew it was not real, she still could not ignore it.

She pulled away from him, immediately ashamed of herself. As she struggled to button up her shirt, Alonna could barely look him in the face. He had not forced her. She'd wanted it. With Ray, he had initially forced her, and then she grew to enjoy it herself. That part she still felt guilty about.

"Can you take me home please? I'm not feeling so well," she said evenly, still looking down and trying to fix her hair.

Shawn, concerned as always, asked "what's wrong? Did I do anything?"

It wasn't his fault, she rationalized. Alonna thought for a moment and wondered if Shawn knew what his touch did to her, and how even his hugs sent her imagination spiraling out of control.

"No," she responded. "You didn't do anything wrong; I just need to get home." If she'd taken heed to Nicole's advice five minutes ago, she would not feel the overwhelming shame she felt at that moment.

She knew that if she was serious about being celibate, she would need to have another conversation with him sooner or later. The conversation would be about responsibility and accountability. She would give him the ultimatum to comply and respect her beliefs, or find someone else. Usually when she would have the conversation, the other person would almost always choose to find someone else, which was, of course, fine with her. In her heart, she knew she probably should have stuck to her guns from the beginning, but there was no way around it now. Shawn Williams had her sprung, and she needed to put the brakes on it.

Shawn, always the gentleman, did not ask any further questions. Rather he helped her put on her jacket, careful not to do anything else to upset her. As she gathered the rest of her belongings, Alonna reminded him to put the dinner in containers so that it did not spoil.

As Shawn drove her back home, he reached over for her hand. Alonna happily complied. She prayed that the talk would not scare him away, as it did the others before

74

him. One thing she had learned from the past was that if it did, that was the clearest way to get a response from God about the potential of the relationship. She hoped He would look favorably on the fact that her heart had not been this happy with another man in years.

****

It had been three days since the incident at his house, and Alonna had screened several of Shawn's calls. The guilt and the shame of her lack of self control still weighed heavily on her. Rather than confront the issue head on, she had allowed the guilt to replay in her mind more times than she could count. Two years of celibacy had almost been lost in a matter of minutes. One of her mother's favorite verses was Matthew 5:14, the one about a light on a hill never being hidden. When she was at the peek of her faith, as she liked to think of it, her actions were dictated by this verse. Preserving her reputation was as important as the air she breathed. She thought back to the night, and the guilt rushed through her mind all over again. Not only had she initiated the moment of passion, but in her heart she'd felt no guilt about wanting it. As a teenager, her mother had advised her about being so hard on herself, and had observed that Alonna sometimes had difficulty forgiving herself for things. As she'd gotten older, it seemed that old habit really was hard to break.

When their relationship started, she knew that it would not be easy, and they both knew that. She'd made light of it instead of having the serious conversation about the vows she'd made. In addition, she purposefully withheld her secrets. Now she wondered how they would be able to build a solid relationship with an already questionable foundation.

Over the past two years, she'd mastered the art of "you never let them see you cry." She'd had her heart broken and she'd managed to break a few herself. If nothing else, she'd learned this from her mother—men love what's hard for them to grasp. She'd perfected the art of being evasive, mysterious, and playing hard to get.

Shawn, however, was different. Their relationship and her level of respect for him was different. Everything in her wanted to call him and apologize, but her stubborn pride would not allow it. It seemed things that she could easily get over in the past, now crippled her. Each day that she did not see her past repeating itself in her present was a success. However, just as those successes were private, so were the struggles. The pattern since the procedure had continued to be two steps forward and three steps back. To explain to Shawn that her guilt was not just about their date, but at the disappointment of reliving what led to the worse decision of her life was inconceivable.

It was already 11am on a Saturday morning, and she was still not out of bed. Although she knew she had a lot to do, it was easier to stay in bed. Shawn had not called her the night before, and she guessed that perhaps he was finally getting tired of her. Alonna looked over at the clock, willing the phone to ring. The minute hand on the clock seemed to be moving at a sluggish speed because each time she checked her phone thinking she'd somehow not heard it ring, she was disappointed to find out that only seconds had gone by. She wondered what he was doing and who he was with. Had they not had a disagreement, she would be working on her project right now.

There's no point crying over spilled milk. Get yourself up!

The only good thing about their split was that she would be able to catch up with Nicole and Ari. Alonna called Ari first.

"Hello," Alonna heard about three rings.

"Hey girl, it's me."

"Well, look who came out of hiding" Ari teased. "Where's Mr. Tall, light and handsome?"

Alonna was not in the mood for joking or small talk. Today, she needed a friend. While she was not yet ready to divulge all of her secrets, she really needed someone to listen to her and assure her that things would be ok.

"We had a fight on Wednesday and kind of broke up," she responded.

"Really?" Alonna could hear the concern in Ari's voice. "What was the fight about, and how do you kind of break up?"

Alonna hadn't meant to break down, but before she knew it she was crying as she recapped the entire incident to Ari.

"Ok. I mean that sounds like a good enough reason for two people to disagree, but how did that lead to an immediate break up?"

Alonna explained that since that night, neither had bothered to call the other.

"I haven't called him because I'm embarrassed." She could not account for why Shawn had not called her, but she could take responsibility for her part. "I made him jump through so many hoops when we first started, and then I threw myself at him with no shame."

77

"Alonna, I know you well enough to know that you don't throw yourself at anyone," Ari said. "I love you, but you are too hard on yourself," she added sternly

Alonna had heard those words before.

"You got caught up. It happens. You would not be human if you never got caught up. This is a reminder of your humanity and desperate need for grace."

Alonna wished she could explain that getting caught up was what led to changes in her life that she dared not tell anyone. She listened patiently to Ari. By the time Ari was finished talking, Alonna felt a lot better. She thanked God for good friends. It was obvious that she cared too much about Shawn to not take responsibility for her actions. Even if he did not accept her apology for reacting abruptly the way she did, she owed it to herself to own up to her choices. Alonna quickly dialed the numbers, before she lost her courage to.

Chapter 11

Things were slowly getting back to normal, and Alonna could not be happier. The weather was unusually warm for a January afternoon, and they decided to take advantage by going for a walk. It was her idea for them to go on a specific route.

She'd picked out the perfect location for The Journey House, and wanted to get his feedback. Throughout the relationship, she'd shared part of her vision, but she knew that unless she was willing to divulge all of her secrets, he probably would not understand the depth of her passion.

When she showed him the building she had in mind, he immediately questioned whether it was a safe location. Alonna knew this would not be the last time someone would question her regarding that, and she had an answer well prepared. She patiently explained that while the area in Southeast DC may not be considered safe by some, it was the perfect location for those she hoped The Journey House would reach. His response was to hug her and kiss her on the forehead to convey his support. Unbeknownst to him, she'd used him as the guinea pig. His reaction would give her an idea of how others, including Nicole and Ari would react. Shawn had approved. He'd understood the vision.

After taking the thirty minute walk back from the building to the train station, Alonna suggested that the two visit her favorite frozen yogurt shop in Arlington. They'd spent the entire day together, but it seemed no matter how much time they spent together, it was never enough. Alonna could talk to him about almost anything, from her irrational fear of cats, to her love for kids, and her decision to recommit to her faith. Even the moments of silence were comfortable.

Alonna sat down in the corner booth of the yogurt shop, enjoying the comfort of being around Shawn as she looked out to the other couples who seemed to be enjoying the same thing.

"I think I love you."

The words came out of nowhere. Alonna looked up, uncertain if she'd even heard him correctly.

Shawn, who was usually the picture of confidence, repeated in a small quiver, "I think I love you."

Since they first met, she'd never heard as much vulnerability in his voice. Alonna searched his eyes intently.

"I think I love you too," she stated looking down.

There were no flashing lights of fireworks like she'd imagined in her mind, but Alonna was relieved. The truth was that since that first fight, she knew she loved him. She fought every urge in her to be the first one to say it. She smiled at her own childish antics.

"When did you know?" She asked sheepishly

"Monday," he said.

Alonna thought back to Monday. She wondered what happened to him on Monday, because to her recollection, their only correspondence was a fifteen minute telephone conversation just before bed because both were exhausted from the weekend.

As if reading her mind, Shawn responded, "Monday was after Sunday. Sunday was when you invited me to church for the first time."

"All the way back then?" Alonna was surprised.

"It did not take me long to realize that you're not just what I want, but also what I need."

Before Alonna could ask him to elaborate, Shawn offered.

"There are things in life that I don't understand, and when I don't understand something, I usually run from it. Even from out first conversation, you would not let me get away with that."

Alonna was surprised by his honesty. Little did he know that, in his own way, he was forcing her to face her own insecurities and fears. Facing things had never come easy to her.

She reached across the table and touched his hand.

"There are things that I just don't understand either. Some things just seem to make much more sense to me through faith."

She could tell that he was still wrestling with the idea of reconciling his past with the things she talked about. While he still did not profess to be one of those evangelical Christians, as he called it, she admired what she believed God was doing in his heart. She sometimes wondered if that was good enough. She could hear her mother's voice, advising her that what she had to compromise to get, she would have to compromise to keep. Alonna ignored that voice. She was finally happy, for the first time in a long time.

She felt his fingers caressing her hand, "I knew on Friday, after I realized that on Thursday I made a mistake." She laughed to herself.

She was referring to their recent argument. Alonna marveled at how being next to him made everything easier. Things felt strangely comfortable. There was a time when this was the standard, and now she constantly had to remind herself that she was worth someone who loved and cherished her. After three months of denial, Alonna had no other choice but to admit that she was in love. Sure, Shawn Williams was funny, intelligent, and respectful, but what she admired most was his kindness. It was no surprise when he revealed over dinner one day that his name meant grace. She silently said a prayer that God will mend his heart, and continue the work of strengthening his faith.

Chapter 12

Something told Alonna when she woke up that today was going to be one of those trying days. She wasn't sure what would happen, but now, as she sat across from the loan officer, she wished she had spent an extra fifteen minutes praying and reading her bible like she usually did. Instead, she'd rushed out of the house, intent on making it to her meeting on time. After running into an unusual amount of traffic on the highway, she ended up being over fifteen minutes late to the meeting. After too much talking, planning, and preparing, today was the day she was to find out if she was approved for a loan to begin renovations on the building for The Journey House.

Just hours earlier, she was confident that with her good credit rating and impeccable business plan, she would be approved for the loan. Now, she sat dumbfounded as she listened to the loan officer explain several reasons why the bank could not approve the loan. He was giving her some ridiculous explanation about the unlikelihood that the work could service the debt. It was not the first time she'd heard a so-called financial expert say that about a startup organization, but she was not buying it. The bank had been recommended by the Small Business Association. The likelihood that she would get approved by another bank was slim to none if this bank did not approve her.

Alonna thought about the many sleepless nights, and the hope that filled her heart whenever she met a child that could benefit from The Journey House. She looked dejectedly at the loan officer as he made copies of the documents detailing why she had been rejected. She'd spent months preparing for this moment, and she knew well that rejection was one of the only two options, but it still stung.

Initially, she'd hoped to avoid the loan process completely. Her ideal situation would include enlisting investors to fund The Journey House—people who could vouch for her idea and her work ethic. However, after many rejections from potential funders, she began to entertain the idea of getting a loan.

Perhaps, God was wrong. Maybe I only heard Him say that The Journey House would be fully funded without any debt.

She tried pleading with the officer and explaining that if the loan was not approved, it would push back approval for everything else including filing other operational documents. The officer remained stone-faced and undaunted by Alonna's requests. By the time the meeting was over, Alonna was drained. It seemed everything she had been working toward for this moment was lost.

As she got in the car to drive home, she could hear Pastor Paul's voice, "delay is not denial."

Sure, Alonna believed that, "but delay still stings," she said to no one in particular as she walked back to her car.

When she woke up that morning, she'd anticipated receiving the news of acceptance, and had plans to celebrate with Nicole and Ari. Now, she was not in the mood for celebrations. She texted both of them and stated that she would rather just spend the evening alone to re-strategize. The meeting with the loan officer had been a short one. She had never been one to give up before, and she was not going to start now. Alonna looked at the clock on the dashboard and saw that it was only 1pm. She would go home and spend the rest of the afternoon researching other funding opportunities. As Alonna put the car into gear, she made a mental note to reach out to her church. Surely, someone of Pastor Paul's caliber knew resources that she probably had not thought of.

****

Hours later, Alonna woke up from an unplanned nap and immediately thought about Shawn. These days he was quickly becoming one of the first things on her mind. She enjoyed their long conversations, and his ability to make her laugh no matter how bleak things appeared. Despite the fact that she thought of him first, she remained diligent about spending time with God during her days. She'd learned the seriousness of God being a jealous God, and vowed to never again put any man before Him; for it was God that had been there before Shawn appeared, and would surely be there if things did not work out, although she prayed fervently that things would work out this time.

After doing her devotional for the day, Alonna picked up her phone to call Shawn. She had been so upset earlier, that she came home and fell asleep without calling to give him the details of the meeting. After only one ring, she heard his voice on the other line.

"Hi, babe," he said.

His voice sent tingles down her spine. Even from a distance, He had that effect on her.

"How are you?" she asked, trying to hide the sadness in her voice. She knew that no matter what he was doing, if he even suspected something was wrong with her, he would immediately come and tend to her, if possible.

"I'm fine babe, I tried to call you earlier, but it kept going to your answering service."

"I'm sorry, I must have turned my phone off," she lied. "What are you doing?"

"I'm just driving to school."

Shawn had decided to begin another Master's program in Engineering during the Spring semester at Georgetown University. When he first told Alonna, she was surprised that he'd managed to go through the application process without telling her. He'd explained that he did not want to get anyone's hopes up, so he kept the process to himself until he received his acceptance. His enrollment in school meant changes to his work schedule, which also affected how frequently they could go out. Despite some disappointment, she was proud of him, and promised to support him.

"Ok. Well, I'm heading out too. I was just thinking about you, so I decided to give you a ring." She lied again.

She knew that he was learning her well enough that if she stayed on the phone any longer, he was sure to pick up on cues about how she was really doing and she just did not have the energy to discuss her day with him.

"A ring huh?" Shawn joked. "I'd like to give you one of those, for sure."

"You know what I meant, silly," she smiled for the first time since she woke up that morning.

"I know, babe. I'm just kidding."

Alonna could hear his smile through the phone.

"I know you're going out with your girlfriends later, so have fun and be safe."

Although she was no longer going out with Nicole and Ari, she could not tell him that either. The questions were sure to begin. She loved how protective he was.

"We'll be alright." Alonna said.

"Listen, I'm going to get off, since I'm sure you don't have your ear piece on and you are driving."

"Ok ma'am. Safety first." Shawn joked.

"Whatever," Alonna joked along with him. "Have a great class, and we'll talk later?"

"Ok, enjoy your time babe."

"Ok, good-bye honey."

Alonna hung up the phone and started to pull the covers back over her head, then decided against it. It seemed that no matter how bleak her circumstances seemed, her two best friends always managed to cheer her up. She'd had enough pity parties for the day. She picked up her phone and texted them, asking that they disregard the first text and meet at their favorite hangout downtown. She had no idea how she would get the funding for The Journey House, but she knew she'd come too far to give up. She was so close, yet things still seemed so far away. Determined not to let things get the best of her, she walked to her closet and picked out her favorite sweater dress. No matter how bad she felt on the inside, a woman always deserved to look her best. Ari had taught her that. Even if she was not feeling good, she would sure look her best for their night out on the town.

Chapter 13

Over dinner the week before, Alonna learned from Nicole that the church had a building they were looking to sell. She'd done some research on her own, and learned that the building was located in Southeast a few miles from the building she had in mind for The Journey House. After finding that out, she immediately set up a meeting with Pastor Paul. Although she'd heard him preach several times, but she'd never met with him one on one. Unsure of how to prepare for the meeting, she'd gone in dressed in a suit, briefcase in hand with documents chronicling all of her work for the center thus far. When she entered his office, she was surprised to see him in jeans and a tee-shirt with little else on his desk than his laptop and a coffee mug.

He was a good-looking man, with an average build and skin the color of cocoa. When he spoke to her, he spoke with a certain confidence, but his voice remained gentle and reassuring. Although she could tell that he was no older than thirty-five, she felt as if she was talking to one of her father's friends.

As they talked, Alonna learned that not only would the church sell the building for a lesser amount than the building she originally had in mind, but they would allow her to use the classrooms in the church, free of charge, for programs while she found independent contractors to work on the building. Since Alonna was still new to the church, Pastor Paul had even gone to the extent of suggesting contractors that were church members that may do the work at a reasonable rate.

Throughout the meeting, she thought about how easy things seemed to be going and recalled the mess that she had experienced with other nonprofits and churches in the past. With humility and candor she explained that she had not planned for The Journey House to be affiliated with the church in any way. Surprisingly, Pastor Paul agreed that once Alonna brought the property, The Journey House would function as an independent entity.

"I don't have a lot of capital for this type of venture. I'm really moving by faith right now," she told him.

His response was a simple, "God will take care of it."

Alonna listened as Pastor Paul discussed ways that the church may be able to consider it an investment that could be repaid over the course of several years. Pastor Paul explained that he would present a rent-to-own proposal to the Board and get back to her within the week about their decision.

She was unsure of why he believed in her vision that much. Perhaps it was what her mother called favor. Regardless of his reason, Alonna walked out of the meeting feeling relieved and quite different from her meetings with the last loan officer.

****

As she watched the last few minutes of *Take the First Dance*, Alonna thought about her relationship with

Shawn. Unlike the characters in the movie, they had not faced much discrimination for being an interracial couple, but she wondered how long that would last. She wondered how her family would react. How would her other friends react once everyone found out they were officially an item?

She'd heard the jokes from Nicole and Ari, but their other friends would not be as gracious. Some would have jokes about how white men can't jump. Others, the more socially conscious type, would lecture her on how "jungle fever" has become the new pandemic—the most serious issue in the black community.

Sure, the times she spent with Shawn were indescribable—the way he made her feel, their great conversations, and most of all, the way he chose to care for her. Alonna knew that none of that would matter to anyone outside of the saved and sanctified people she went to church with. All they would think about is that he was a white man, and she was a good black woman who had gotten caught up in a supposed system. A gorgeous white man he was, but a white man nonetheless. They would ask what kind of life experiences and struggles he had to share.

Her father would ask why she could not find a suitable Black man at Howard. Sure, Grace would only care about whether he was able to buy her nice things and protect her like the big brother she'd always wanted, but her father was the biggest problem. She would have to be intentional to bring up all the wonderful things about him that she had come to respect and admire.

It was only Wednesday, but as she thought about their plans for the weekend, Alonna wondered whether the barrage of questioning that was sure to come was worth it. They would be attending a Valentine's Day party at Tony, a former classmate's house on Saturday.

While she was gone in Chicago, Nicole and Ari had continued their friendship with Tony who also stayed in the area. When the four were in college, he was like a big brother to the three of them. At one point, Alonna suspected that he may have been interested in her, but by then, their relationship was resting comfortably in the friend zone. With Tony, there was never a dull moment. Alonna was sure that Saturday would be a night to remember.

Alonna felt the vibration of her phone next to her computer and quickly reached for the phone.

"Hello?"

"Hey, how are you?" asked the deep, masculine voice.

"I'm fine. I was just thinking about you," she smiled, "how are you?"

"I'm doing great. I was thinking about you too," Shawn said. "I was trying to find out what you wanted to eat for dinner; I'll just pick up something on my way after work."

Alonna was learning how not to take even the simplest gestures for granted.

"Shawn, that is so sweet. Thank you."

"No problem, honey."

She requested the chicken salad dinner from Island Delight, a restaurant that was quickly becoming one of their favorites as a couple.

She thought back to when she was dating Ray and she was in bed, sick, for a week. During that time, he came to her apartment two times to check on her. She remembered lying on the couch and wondering where he was, if he was not at her apartment checking on her. During the six days that she was sick and unable to cook or clean, he never even once offered to bring her dinner, to help her clean or do other daily chores. She thought about Shawn, and thanked God for the difference. With him, she'd only briefly mentioned that she wasn't feeling well, and throughout the day she'd received several phone calls with him just checking on her.

"Baby girl, did you hear me?"

She liked when he called her that, mainly because the only other man in the world who ever referred to her as that was her father, during the good days.

"No, I'm sorry. I got distracted. What did you say?" She asked.

"Are you ok? If you're not feeling any better I could leave work early" Ray offered.

"Sweetheart, that's ok," Alonna said, "I'm fine."

"Ok, well then I should be at your place around six o'clock. I'll be leaving here around five O'clock today."

"That's fine honey," Alonna said sweetly, "I will see you then."

"Ok, call me if you need anything, ok?"

"Ok." Alonna paused. "Shawn?"

"Yes?"

"Thank you."

"You're welcome sweetie," Shawn answered. "Alonna, you know you mean a lot to me right?"

"I'm starting to believe that" Alonna smiled.

"Good. See you in a few hours."

Alonna hung up the phone. She looked at the clock showing 1pm, and realized she now only had three more hours to complete the initial program curriculum she was working on. After that she'd have to take a shower, and then try to muster enough strength to do some long overdue cleaning of her apartment, and make herself look decent for

92

her man. She could hardly believe it, but she, Alonna Jones, had a man. "And Shawn Williams is my man," she said out loud to no one in particular. She was proud of their relationship, and she decided that on Saturday and any other day, no one else's opinion would matter.

Alonna chuckled and thought "if things work out, at least my last name will still be nice." No sooner did she think that, she shook her head at the idea of marrying someone else. The wound from Ray was just beginning to heal, and she wondered if she would let anyone else get that close to it again. She loved Shawn, no doubt about it, but marriage plans would have to wait, for now.

****

The party had started at 7:30, but at the last minute Alonna decided to change her outfit. When she finally decided on a form-fitting, knee-length red and black dress, she noticed what Shawn was wearing and asked that he change it. Despite his resistance, she insisted that they stop at the closest department store to purchase a new tie. She knew her college friends enough to know that in these types of situation, first impressions were everything. For them, tonight's party was the equivalent of a high school reunion. Although she generally did not care what other people said, she did not want to give any fodder for gossip either. If they say nothing else, her friends could at least say that they are a good-looking and well-dressed couple. She shook her head as she realized that after ten years of friendship, Nicole's ways were definitely rubbing off on her.

After the one hour detour to the nearest Macy's, and standing in lines full of men who were hustling to buy last-minute valentine's day gifts for their partners, Shawn and Alonna finally arrived at Tony's. By the time they pulled up his driveway, it was almost 9 O'clock. The music could be heard from down the street, which is where Alonna and Shawn had to park because there were so many cars on what looked like a usually quiet suburban street. From the conversations she'd had with Nicole and Ari, it seemed that everyone who was anyone had an invitation to this party.

There was no better time than now to officially introduce him to the rest of her acquaintances and friends. For months, she'd managed to keep her worlds apart, and every time someone probed to find out who she was dating, she'd successfully dodged the question. Rumors had started to spread, and she was determined to address them today. She had to admit that the more time she spent with Shawn, she more impressed she was, even if no one else would be.

The man cleaned up nice, she thought as she straightened his tie one last time. She was relieved that, even if for one night only, he managed to ditch his usual uniform of khakis and sweaters, for a black slacks and a red polo shirt that fit his physique perfectly. Alonna thought for a second. Perhaps if the lights were dim enough, no one would notice that he was white.

Get over yourself!

She chided herself. She smiled wryly at her own absurd idea. As they walked hand in hand to Tony's house, she channeled the confidence that she once possessed, held her chest out, and turned the knob to enter the house.

****

She had envisioned a low pressure environment where her friends and acquaintances would be too busy to give Shawn a hard time. Two hours later, she found that what she got, instead, was a platform for the world to take note about her new relationship. Despite the fact that she'd clung to Shawn, it seemed people swarmed around him all night. Perhaps it was because he was one of the few people who were not black at the party, or because he turned out to know more people than she did. Either way, she was tired of standing on her feet in the four inch heels that she was wearing. She found a nice quiet corner to sit and relax on Tony's patio. It seemed Spring was planning on making an early entrance. She sipped her glass of wine and stared out at the skyline that seemed perfectly created for the occasion.

"So, this is where you've been hiding."

She turned around to see Nicole holding out her black shoulder wrap. She'd been too mesmerized by the night sky and the soothing quiet of being outside to move. She took the scarf, thankfully.

"It seems lover boy is a hit tonight," Nicole said, resting her back against the patio railing.

"Tell me about it! Who would've thought it?" Alonna exclaimed.

"Definitely not me," Nicole joked. "Although I will admit that he has the tall and handsome part down. The dark part, not so much," she added.

Alonna had long accepted Nicole's sometimes off-putting sense of humor. Not everyone would appreciate it, but that's why they were best friends. The two laughed about the incident as Alonna recapped the irony in finding out that not only did Shawn not need a babysitter all evening, but he was actually turning into the life of the party.

"He's been so caught up in keeping his fans happy, that he probably doesn't even know I'm out here." Alonna laughed.

She enjoyed that about Shawn. He was a social chameleon of sorts. No matter the setting, he adapted well. He'd adapted so well tonight, that it seemed that the last thing on most people's mind was their relationship.

"So, what about your girl Vickie?" Nicole asked, as she sat down next to Alonna to keep an eye on the party going on inside.

"What about her?" Alonna asked with a little bit more sass than she'd intended to.

She knew Nicole was asking about their exchange earlier, but Alonna was trying to be the better person. Nicole gave her a knowing look, asking her to spill the beans. They both knew that since college, Vickie had tried her best to be Alonna's rival. She'd participated in many of the same activities that Alonna did, and was always trying to outdo her.

For a time Alonna had given in and played along, determined not be outdone by someone with the likes of Vickie Richardson. However, by senior year, Alonna had given up the battle, after realizing that with people like her, the competition never ends. With plans to accept a job offer in another state, she had no room for continuing on in a silly competition anyway.

When she and Shawn first walked in to Tony's house, she hadn't noticed Vickie. She'd spoken to everyone that crossed their path, and cordially introduced Shawn to those who did not know him. Within a matter of minutes, he was the one introducing Alonna to those he knew from local lounges, the gym, or any of the thousands of social events that frequently occurred in the active Washington

96

DC metro area. Of the many people that came up to Shawn to say hello, Alonna immediately noticed Vickie. Determined not to get caught up in any of her childish antics, Alonna held on to her man's hand and gave it a squeeze. She relaxed as she observed that Shawn paid no attention to Vickie.

"I saw her over there talking to you. Are you guys best friends again?" Nicole laughed.

"Well, she came over to us as if we were best friends." Alonna recapped how Vickie had walked over to her and Shawn, and in her typical style, dramatically gave her a hug and loudly flattered her with compliments.

"Why would she do that?"

"I think she was trying to get Shawn's attention."

"So, she's switching over to the other side too?" Nicole laughed at her own joke.

Alonna gave her a teasing shove.

"Shawn didn't pay her any attention, of course." Alonna smiled.

"Of course not. You know that imitation is still the highest form of flattery." Nicole reached her arm across her friend's shoulder.

"With all seriousness, I really like him for you, Loni."

Alonna squeezed her friend's hand. This was the first time that Nicole had said that out loud, and the validation meant a lot to her.

"Thanks a lot, Nik," she said as she wrapped the sarong tighter around her shoulders.

"So, you guys are partying without me huh?" Their conversation was interrupted as Ari came bursting through the patio door.

"Never without you," Nicole responded, patting the empty chair on her other side.

"I see prince charming is a hit." Ari looked over at Alonna teasingly.

"So to Nik, he's lover boy, and to you, he's prince charming?" Alonna asked.

"I'll take it," she added.

"I've been watching him over the last couple of hours, and I really like him for you," Ari added.

Nicole looked at her knowingly. "It's confirmation," she said with a wink.

Ari looked at the two with a slight look of confusion. "Anyway, I saw your girl Vickie trying to get up in his face."

Alonna retold the entire story to Ari, as the three laughed and traded stories. It was only when Ari commented that it was getting too chilly outside that they decided to rejoin the rest of the party.

Alonna spotted Shawn in the living room. He was talking to the same guy that she left him with when she'd went out to the patio an hour earlier. Judging from how animated the two were, she assumed they may have been talking about sports. She walked up to him quietly and sat down next to him on the couch. Almost instinctively, he placed his arm around her. It was getting late, but she stayed there, enjoying the moment.

Chapter 14

Alonna woke up, and was slightly disturbed. She could not shake the feeling that the dream left her with. It wasn't a scary dream, but it seemed all too real. She knew that it had some meaning to her, but could not understand what it meant.

In the dream, she woke up and realized that her two front and bottom teeth had rotted away. In the dream, there was no process, but rather it appeared her teeth had rotted away over night. She recalled being extremely fearful of what other people would think after seeing her reflection. Her reaction seemed appropriate, especially because she wore braces for so long, and her smile had become her signature.

In her real life, Alonna paid a great deal of attention to her teeth, and followed her dentist's recommendations closely. She loved having a nice and clean smile. Alonna remembered that in the dream, she looked in the mirror and was saddened that her perfect smile no longer existed, and unlike a broken tooth, she could not fix or mask a rotten and discolored tooth. It was there for all to see. In the dream, Alonna began to interact with her friends, and to her surprise no one commented on her rotten teeth. She was sure that they noticed, but everyone continued with their interactions as they had in the past. It seemed that only to Alonna was her smile compromised. In her mind's eye, she could see that her smile was tarnished, but there was something oddly inviting about it. Although an adult in the dream, her new smile made her appear child-like, like a young girl, waiting for her adult teeth to come in.

She'd been so disturbed by the dream that she woke up with night sweats. She had been advised to write her dreams down numerous times, and rarely did she do it, but today Alonna took out her journal. She frantically wrote down all the details she could remember about this dream that she was sure spoke symbolically of her life in some way. As she wrote, she prayed that she would receive some kind of revelation and insight in to the meaning of the dream.

After writing down the dream, she could not go back to sleep, so Alonna continued with her morning routine as usual. Today, she would have breakfast at home, while doing her devotional, before heading downtown to meet with the contractors for The Journey House. Of the four men that Pastor Paul recommended, two had agreed to combine their resources in order to complete the work on the building in time for a Fall grand opening.

No sooner did she begin her morning devotion, Alonna received the revelation that her heart needed. She was reminded about the thing that she feared others finding out. The thing that, if anyone found out, was sure to cause friends to walk away in shame and embarrassment of ever associating with her. As she wrote down the revelation that she was receiving, a new peace filled her. It would have been hard to explain to anyone who was not spiritual, but Alonna could almost feel the hand of God as He comforted her that while she cannot get back what she lost, He was changing everything to reflect the power of redemption. Alonna cried. The rotting teeth were her blemish, but the crippling fear that others would notice was a lie from Satan himself. Not only did others not treat her any differently, but what she perceived as a blemish, others somehow saw as beautiful.

Alonna cried as peace washed over her. She realized she had been doing that a lot as of late, but it seemed to be the only appropriate response for such a heavy revelation given through a simple dream that she thought was just about teeth. It was the first time in three years that she'd felt any peace associated with the burden she carried. Alonna breathed a sigh of relief, knowing that when the time for her to display her fears and challenges, her creator had already comforted her that all will be well.

Alonna was alert as she realized that this may mean that the opportunity to display her fear was coming soon. With the creation of The Journey House, she knew it would not be long before she would feel compelled to share her story with someone—most likely one of the teens that would come to the center seeking refuge from life's turmoil. She'd long known that she would be involved with working with teenagers and underserved people, and experience had taught her that with some, transparency was the only way to gain their trust. The feeling was bitter sweet. She'd prayed for this opportunity, but she wondered if the cost was too high.

The peace that was flooding her left no room for resentment, bitterness or doubt. She had to face her choices. She only prayed that the Lord would hold her up to face the consequences of those choices, whatever those consequences may be, and no matter how long after the choice was made. She'd spent so many nights crying because the guilt of it all weighed down on her so heavily. Today, she was not crying because of guilt, but relief from the assurance that she would be ok. She vowed never to make a mistake like that again. She would never allow anyone or anything take her back to that filthy place of shame.

Chapter 15

True to his word, Pastor Paul presented Alonna's ideas to the Board, and they quickly approved her plans. According to Pastor Paul, they had been eagerly waiting for a community program, but they lacked the manpower to execute it. For that reason alone, they vowed to fully support her work with The Journey House.

Within weeks, the first phase of her plan was put into effect—small community groups to gauge interest from the local teenagers. The groups would meet weekly, and they would be led by local college students looking to satisfy their community service hours.

As she listened to this week's group session, Alonna thought about how much they reminded her of her and her friends during their teenage years. So much had happened in such a short time, and as she observed the class, she thanked God that the teens in the community now had one more resource to support them.

On this particular day, her attention was drawn out to one specific girl. The small group had only been meeting for three weeks, but the class seemed to double in size with new girls coming each week. Some girls were there because their parents were making them come, and others were coming voluntarily because they were desperately seeking the support system that they did not have at home.

As Alonna looked at the girl, she could not figure out which group she belonged in. The girl reminded her a little bit of Grace because she seemed a bit awkward, but she was still one of the most beautiful girls in the group. Her awkwardness conveyed to Alonna, that she was probably not aware of how remarkable her features were. Her skin was the color of the coffee beans that Alonna would help her grandmother roast during her summers down south. Her hair was coarse, and Alonna admired the creative pattern of braids that ran down her back. Although Alonna only saw her smile once during the one hour the group had already being going on, it was one of the most captivating smiles she'd ever seen. The gap between her teeth only seemed to make her smile more distinct. At first glance, the girl appeared to be shy and introverted, but Alonna knew better. She recognized the curiosity in her eyes, and the way she sat up whenever someone talked about a topic that interested her. For some reason, she never spoke up.

Two hours later, the room was clean and most of the girls were gone. Alonna noticed the girl as she helped the volunteer instructor rearrange the classroom back to its original order. The girl worked attentively, but her thoughts seemed to be in another world. Alonna walked over to her.

"Hello there."

Upon noticing Alonna standing next to her, the teen took the headphones out of her ears.

"Sorry about that, ma'am. I was listening to my favorite singer, Ledell. Her songs are so deep. She actually just won best new female Christian artist of the year." The girl motioned for Alonna to look at her IPod, which showed a picture of a beautiful brown skinned girl with a stunning smile, and soft afro curls holding a guitar over her shoulder. Since she'd heard about Ledell from Grace as well, Alonna made a mental note to check out the singer when she got home that evening.

"Anyway, please excuse my rudeness. Good evening ma'am," the girl said, extending her hand toward Alonna

Alonna was both surprised and impressed. "I'm Alonna. What's your name? I haven't seen you here before." Alonna extended her hand, which was met by a confident and firm grip.

"Wait a minute," the girl paused. "Are you Alonna Jones, the one that's building the center down the street for the program?" Alonna could hear the excitement in her voice. Had she not known any better, she would have thought the girl was mistaking her for a national celebrity. Alonna nodded and smiled politely.

"Nice to meet you, Ms. Alonna. Yes, this is my first time. My name is Renee and my mother and I just moved here from North Carolina. She heard about this from her coworker and made me come."

Alonna chuckled at the girl's attempt to remain polite despite her contempt for being forced to come.

"Well, what did you think?"

"About tonight? I thought it was great. I learned a lot. I wish the other kids were friendlier though. No one even came up to me to ask me my name or anything. Other than that, it was great."

Alonna smiled, "you don't hold back much huh?"

Renee laughed heartily. Alonna took note that not only was Renee not shy, but she was quite confident and comfortable in her own skin. She envied the boldness the young girl, and she could not shake the feeling that she reminded her so much of herself.

"Are you going to come back?" she asked.

"Yes, ma'am. I had a great time."

Alonna shook her head, "if you're going to come back, you must learn the first rule."

"What's that?" Renee asked.

"No calling me ma'am. Ok?"

Renee smiled, "yes, Ms. Alonna."

Alonna laughed. There was something quite quirky but likeable about this girl. When she first got the idea for The Journey House, she'd envisioned the thousands of Renees in the world that she could work closely with. She would make herself available as a resource for them, because she knew how hard the teenage years could be. It was only by God's grace that she'd made it through the way she did. Alonna wondered what this girl's story was, because like every other young person that was coming to the program, she had to have some sort of backstory.

"Ma..I mean Ms. Alonna?"

Renee's voice startled Alonna back to the moment.

"Yes, Ms. Renee?"

Renee laughed that contagious laugh of hers. "I was just asking if there's anything else I can do, because I think my mother is outside?"

"No ma'am. Thank you for all of your help. I'll see you next week."

"Ok, see you next week," and with that the young girl started jogging away and waving to Alonna. Overall, the night had gone very well she thought as she stacked the remaining chairs in the classroom.

Chapter 16

Thursday made the second week in a row that they had been unable to make their usual date night. Shawn had cited upcoming finals as the reason, and while Alonna wanted to be supportive of his pursuits, she could not help but be disappointed. She, too, had been having rough week because the work for The Journey House was taking longer than expected, which meant that inspection would have to be pushed back another month. She looked forward to the time she and Shawn spent together, because other than Nicole and Ari, he was the only one that understood the intricacies of the process. He was her sounding board.

Because they had been unable to make their usual date night, Shawn had planned an elaborate dinner tonight to make up for it. With him, Alonna sometimes worried that things may be too good to be true. She'd long learned to ignore the feelings that she was compromising. How could something that felt so right be wrong?

Within the last month, Shawn had stopped going to church with her like he'd promised. He often cited school as his reason for that too. However, Alonna surmised that what he lacked in faith, he made up for in consideration, gentleness and an awareness of her needs.

Once, when she'd confided in her mother about how Ray was treating her, her mother had advised her that no matter how hard a man tried, without the love of God, he was incapable of loving a woman. That did not seem to be the case for Shawn. He avoided all things pious, but he seemed the most aware partner of anyone she'd ever been with.

****

The make-up date was spectacular. Alonna was still surprised that he somehow remembered that on their first date, she talked about wanting to go to a new and very expensive Thai restaurant. She'd talk about how she loved ethnic foods, especially Thai food. Shawn had surprised her by making reservations to the restaurant, which was in Baltimore, and then purchasing tickets for a local cruise around the Baltimore harbor.

As they sat parked in front of her house, she could hardly believe it. It had been some time since any man had put that much thought into a date with her. She was impressed that five months into their relationship, he was still working hard to impress her. Not only that, not once, since the first incident, had he tried to cross her boundaries. By now, he knew well her vow of celibacy.

Their ride back to her house had been a quiet one, as Alonna thought about ways that she could thank him for his effort and consideration. As he walked her to her door, she felt his arm across her shoulder. Alonna loved the feeling of being protected under his care. She gently removed his arm from her shoulder and teasingly led him to the front door. It was a cool night, and Alonna just wanted to enjoy his company. As Alonna fumbled with the keys, Shawn bent over and kissed her on the cheek.

"Want to watch a movie?" she looked up at him longingly.

108

"Baby girl, I still have exams next week. It's probably not the best idea."

"Please?" Alonna pleaded. Sure, they had spent all evening together, but with him, the time seemed to go by too quickly.

Shawn shook his head, but Alonna was determined not to take no for an answer.

"Are you not spending time with me because you're spending it with someone else?" She asked accusingly.

She noticed the look of disappointment that was quickly replaced by a knowing smile.

As he sat down on the couch, Alonna could hear him call out behind her, "we can hang out, but only for an hour."

"I'll take an hour. I can't believe I have to beg my boyfriend to spend time with me," she shouted from her room as she changed out of the sweater dress she was wearing.

"You make me feel so wanted," he teased back.

Alonna went over to where he was sitting on the couch, bent over and gave him a kiss and walked toward the kitchen. Minutes later, she came back with a bottle of water for Shawn, and a glass of lemonade for herself. She had changed into more comfortable clothes, and sat snuggled next to him on the couch. She'd seen the movie they decided on countless times, but the comfort and warmth of being next to him was all that mattered.

As she lay on the couch with her head resting on his legs, she could feel his hands massaging her back. She leaned up and kissed him on the lips. The kisses started gently at first, but it seemed each kiss grew more passionate and more intense. Before she knew it, the kissing had turned into caressing. All of which felt great to

Alonna's body. An internal war was waging. She knew the consequences of pushing the boundaries. Twice she had paid for it with blood, and once they nearly separated because of it. However, the warmth of Shawn's breath and the caress of his touch seemed to be exactly what her body was craving.

You have had a stressful week. Just look at it as much-deserved relief.

Shawn seemed to know his way around her body perfectly. Without any guidance from her, his hands made their way to her bra strap, as his lips gently kissed her neck. As her clothes fell off her body, the warmth of his body became as a magnet drawing her closer to him. Shawn removed his shirt, and started in on Alonna's pants. Alonna tried to move his hand away, but each time they seemed to find their way back around her body.

Unlike the last time when she was able to call everything to a complete stop, Alonna had no desire to end things this time. Her body craved his, and from the way his strong hands made their way from her neck to her back to her chest, it was clear that he was craving her as well. As Shawn slipped out of his pants, she led him to her room, and in a matter of moments, everything she'd vowed to for three years slipped away.

As they sat up in her bed, Alonna held her head in her hands sobbing.

Shawn pulled the covers up on her, as he gently kissed her back.

"What's wrong?" He asked.

It was clear to Alonna that he'd envisioned a much happier reaction to their first night together. He'd joked before that he'd never gotten complaints before, and smirked at the notion that if they ever got to that point, she would definitely enjoy it.

Alonna drew away from him quickly and snapped, "I knew it! I knew that you were only after me because you wanted it."

"What are you talking about?" Shawn responded with a look of confusion.

He reached for her again, and again she drew back.

"You are just like every other man! You have bad intentions, and you think you can find one more victim for your hit it and quit it ploy!" Alonna was furious. "You think that because you brought me a nice dinner and spent a few dollars on me that gives you the right to take advantage of me?"

For a few seconds, Shawn looked to Alonna like Ray. They were not the same person, but the image of the man who'd caused her to lose everything was forever etched in her mind.

"Loni, you were the one that brought me in here. You started kissing me," Shawn responded meekly. "I'm sorry if I went with it, but I am a human being too," He responded.

Alonna could hear a slight hurt in his voice, but his feelings were irrelevant to her.
She wrapped the sheets around her body and stormed to the door.

"Get out" she demanded.

"Alonna, think about this. We both went a little too far. Let's just talk about this. I thought we got past this last time," he pleaded.

"I said get out," she seethed through clenched teeth.

She had never talked to him like that before, but things had gone too far, and there was nothing she could do

111

about it now. She'd vowed to celibacy, and kept her promise for over three years, and within minutes, it was all destroyed. Alonna could handle the frustration, but the guilt was the worst part. How could she preach to young girls about knowing their worth and keeping themselves pure, when she was incapable of doing so herself?

Shawn picked up his jacket and walked dejectedly toward the door. It seemed he was going to make one more remark, but before he could, Alonna slammed the bedroom door in his face.

She turned her back against the door and slid down and wept. Not since her last visit to the clinic had she wept like this. It seemed the very things she did not want to do, and knew not to do, were the things she kept on doing.

She was angry with Shawn for not stopping her from wanting the things that she did, and angry at herself for holding him to an unfair standard. Minutes later she heard him closing the front door to her apartment. She slowly made her way to the couch, and picked up the trail of clothes she'd left on the floor. She reached for her robe, the first thing that had come off, and wrapped it tightly around her body and curled up on the couch. She mourned for innocence lost, and for her inability to learn from her mistakes. She mourned because it seemed that the best thing that'd happened to her in the last three years just walked out of her life, and perhaps for good this time.

Chapter 17

No matter how hard she tried, she could not stop the tears. Alonna had not known guilt like this in a while. Even the immediate guilt from the procedure was not comparable. At least then, she'd justified everything by saying that the alternative was too costly. An unplanned pregnancy before marriage would mean her reputation would have been tarnished, her parents would have been humiliated, and Ray would be irate. To save them all, she'd made the right decision, she rationalized. Now, she had no excuse.

She remembered how her mother used to say "when you know better, you do better." She'd known better. She'd made this commitment to herself in her new zeal for the supposed righteous things that she heard about in church. She could not help but think that now she was one of the hypocrites that everyone, including Shawn and her father, talked about.

She remembered how two months earlier, when she and Shawn had gotten really close, she'd cried herself to sleep asking that this time, she would get it right.

Alonna thought back to the night before. She could not remember what stirred her desire and led to the incident. Neither one of them had intentionally indulged in anything that would lead to that end result, but somehow they'd managed to lose all inhibitions and participated in the forbidden. Almost instantly, Alonna knew that five minutes of pleasure had not been worth it. When she thought about it, she laughed cynically because the pleasure had turned out to be not so pleasurable as the mood had been dampened by the guilt that she felt. She instantly became resentful at Shawn for taking joy in her weakness. She'd been told that all men need it. She believed that it was part of God's plan that it be enjoyable. However, the guilt of taking it out of context was unbearable.

She'd cried herself to sleep the night before, and this morning she'd woken up intent on moving on with her life. She thought about how much time she'd wasted being mad at Ray. She was not going to repeat the same thing with Shawn. After taking a shower, Alonna grabbed her IPod off the kitchen counter. She hoped a morning jog would help to lift her mood. She knew that, as had become their morning routine, any minute Shawn would be calling to say good morning and to check on her. The last thing she needed was to hear his voice, so she left her phone by the bible she'd tried, but failed at, reading earlier.

With barely enough strength to stand up, Alonna walked to the door. Today would likely not be a jogging day, but a slow, contemplative walk day.

****

Spring was just starting, and the cool air was exactly what Alonna needed. She loved the sound of birds chirping, and the first trace of the cherry blossoms that lined the jogging path by her home. Almost a year ago, she'd made this journey back, anxious and anticipating a new beginning, only to find herself right back at where she started.

Alonna put her headphones in her ears. The latest India Arie album was exactly what the doctor ordered. She'd listened to that album hundreds of time, and each time India's raspy voice, soothing melodies, and affirming lyrics would energize her to face whatever her challenge was at the moment. By the time she looked down at her watch, she noticed that she had been walking for fifteen minutes. The fresh air was definitely doing a lot for her mood.

What do you do the morning after a slip, and the guilt is too much, so you just shout, asking the Lord to redeem?

The lyrics were unfamiliar to Alonna. As she looked down at her IPod, she noticed that the artist was not India Arie, but rather a male rapper. Always a sucker for the fresh sound that results from the pairing of a rapper and songstress, Alonna decided to listen to the song. She assumed that Grace must have downloaded the song during her last visit to her parents. Ten minutes later Alonna found herself sitting on the bench and pressing repeat for the third time.

The song was by a new Christian rapper featuring Ledell. Although she secretly doubted whether He still cared, it seemed that somehow God had divinely orchestrated for the song to make it to her India Arie playlist just for her to hear this morning.

Alonna, undaunted by the curious stares onlookers, sobbed at the subtle reminder of God's grace for her. Almost instantly, Alonna remembered Psalm 51. It had been one of the first Psalms that she remembered reading and referencing as a new Christian. Her favorite line in the scripture had always been "a broken and contrite heart He will not despise." She could not remember a recent time when she was more broken than she felt today. For the fourth time in a row, she heard the rapper in the background singing.

What do you do the morning after a slip, and the guilt is too much, so you just shout, asking the Lord to redeem?

As if singing the anthem to her life, the rapper continued. Alonna continued to let the tears flow. Tears at the gentle reminder that her identity is made new as a result of her repentance. And it seemed almost instantly a new kind of peace washed over Alonna, as it replaced the feelings of worry, insecurity, and guilt. Alonna got up from the bench, and louder than she anticipated because of the headphones in ears, she said to no one in particular, "hello, new mercies." She pressed repeat one more time, as she walked one more lap around the path.

****

She remembered the conversation she had with Charles Johnson on his graduation day. With more emotion than she'd ever seen before, he had told her she was different. He confided to Alonna that he converted to Christianity because he saw her live out her faith, unlike the other hypocrites he knew. She'd found joy in knowing that her walk played a part in that. She quietly thanked God, but the thought made her even sadder now as she realized how far she had come. She remembered the Wednesday morning her life changed forever.

Alonna rolled over on the bed as she recalled the conversation. She'd picked up the phone and called him,

116

hoping that he would comfort her and make it all go away. As quickly as she said the words "I'm pregnant," she regretted it. At that point, there was no need for small talk.

"Another scare?" she heard him ask disdainfully as if she'd become pregnant by herself.

"Yes," she replied ignoring the contempt in his voice, "and I need some money."

"Fine, I get paid next week. We can take care of it then."

Take care of it.

The words ran in her ears. That night, she'd angrily hung up the phone and wept. How could she have gotten to a place of falling for a man who lacked the conviction to even think twice about such a decision?

She thought back to how she was well-known on her college campus for her uncompromising values. She had unintentionally formed a reputation as a girl that was hard to get and would not hesitate to turn a guy down if she even suspected his motives were wrong. She questioned what those efforts were for. Could she have been doomed from the beginning?

She thought back to her first visit to the clinic; the cold walls, the cold staff, and the secrecy. The secrecy was the most exhausting part. With the exception or herself, Ray, and God, no one had ever known her secret. After she finally gotten the nerve to set up the appointment, following through became a covert operation.

Her first visit was at 6am on a Saturday morning. She'd worn a sweater on the July morning because no matter what she did, she could not shake the chill in her body. Thankful for her sweater, she used it to cover her face, for fear of being spotted by someone who knew her. She knew that any one of the protesters outside could be a

117

member of her church or any number of ministries she belonged to. If anyone found out, that would be the end of her. Her parents would be too embarrassed to react, her friends too shocked to judge. Even to her, the idea was shocking. It seemed she was having an out of body experience. The most unbelievable part for Alonna was that this was the second time in four months.

The first time, she lost the baby due to supposed natural causes, although Alonna suspected that stress led to that. Since that day, there were times she stood up for hours, awake, thinking about the events of the past years that had forever changed the story of her life. Her life had drastically changed ways she never planned or imagined. This night was no different. The weight of what she had done, the odor of the clinic was as real to her as the day she went through with her decision.

Feeling too guilty to walk to her prayer closet, all she could do was weep. Weep for the blood on her hands, and for the weight of decisions that can never be undone.

You'll never have another.

God will never forgive you.

How can you call yourself a Christian, knowing you took a life? All you are is a big hypocrite.

No man will ever want you when they find out how cold and used you are.

The accusations rang loud in her ears. She longed for freedom and healing.

That kind of healing only comes from confession and repentance.

This time the voice was no accusing her, but it was a calm and welcoming voice. She had to tell someone, and she knew the day was going to come sooner than later. Her freedom was depending on it, and it was long overdue.

Chapter 18

It had been two months since their argument, and while there were some days she only thought about Shawn a few times during the day, most times she missed him terribly. Initially she'd hoped that Shawn would call her so they could talk about what happened, but the more she thought about the incident, the more she realized about herself—the recurring breakdowns were an indication of some unresolved issues in her life. She was tired of running, and if she needed to spend some time alone to work through those issues, that's what she would do.

The reality though was that even when she and Ray had called off the wedding, Alonna hadn't felt this bad. Then, at least, she knew with little doubt that she'd made the right decision after giving all of herself to someone who did not appreciate her. With Shawn, she could never be completely sure. With him there was always something urging her to hang in there. She'd asked him to leave her life out of frustration, but deep in her heart, she grieved the loss. She'd learned not to base decisions on emotions, but this feeling was unbearable. There were days she hoped that he would call one last time to work things out, but she knew he wouldn't.

His pride was hurt, and her mother always taught her that there is nothing more dangerous than a man with hurt pride. Her pride was hurt too though, and two prideful people made for bad partners in a relationship. She'd credited that lesson to Ray as well.

Lately it seemed things were becoming too skewed for her comfort. Ray and Shawn, the lines that separated the two were becoming blurred. That night, Shawn had reminded her of Ray, and she hated every single minute of it. The idea of a repeat of that relationship made her blood boil. He'd asked her to trust him, and she had. She had given him the benefit of the doubt, but did he have to touch her like that? She feared that the respect was lost and she had contributed to that. Today was a rough day, because all attempts to push thoughts of Shawn aside were unsuccessful. Alonna wondered what he was doing. Was he hurt too? Did he call any of the girls that seemed to be constantly vying for his attention? After the way she treated him, she was sure that he'd moved on. That was fine because knowing that would confirm that he was like the rest of them and she had made a good decision. However, no matter how many times she told herself that, it still hurt.

****

Alonna said a series of expletives in her head. When she'd strayed away from the church, cursing was one of the bad habits she'd picked up. Occasionally, when things got out of control, she found herself resorting back to that old habit. Sure it was a nice April day, but this was not the way she intended on enjoying the outdoors. Something had told her she should have fixed the tire when she could. Instead,

120

she'd chosen to spend the few hours she had last Saturday picking out furniture for her new office.

As she paced around the car on the side of Highway 295, she reasoned that she could go over the budget on the phone with the accountant while she waited for someone who come to her aid. At this rate, she was going to be over one hour late for their meeting.

When she was with Shawn, things like that could be taken care of very quickly. When they broke up, she'd had to find a new mechanic, and although he kept her car running well, she hated the smell of the shop, and the way he managed to turn polite banter into inappropriate innuendos.

Here she was stuck on the side of the Baltimore-Washington Parkway at three o'clock in the afternoon. The rush hour traffic would soon begin to pile up, and the nightmare was only certain to get worse if she did not find someone to help her.

Alonna sighed and thought about who she could call to come rescue her. She'd tried everyone she knew would be willing to help her. She'd tried to call Ari, but she had not picked up her telephone. At this time of the day on a Monday afternoon, she was most likely in a meeting. After dialing Nicole's number, she quickly hung up, remembering that she was out of town at a conference. She'd tried her cousin Mike, but he could not get away from his shop long enough to make the trip. When things were tight financially she could not renew her Triple "A" membership, and eventually she just forgot about it. Alonna tried to call three other friends, all of whom were either stuck with a project, or were at an important appointment, and would not be able to rescue her for some hours. She could hear her stomach growling. There's no way she could wait on the side of the parkway for a few hours. Besides her stomach gnawing at itself, Alonna thought about last week's episode of *1000 Ways to Die,* in which a young girl pulled over on the side of the road was rammed into by a tractor trailer after one of its wheels was freakishly detached. The girl's car was pushed over the rail and landed on the roadway underneath.

Alonna quickly dialed her accountant's number to cancel the meeting. Thankfully, he was understanding, but even he could not come to rescue her since his office was across town.

She put her head down, took in a deep breath, and dialed the numbers that she was dreading having to dial.

"Hello" she heard after one ring.

"Hi," Alonna answered weakly.

"Is everything ok?" He didn't even bother to make small talk. He knew her very well. Alonna could hear the alarm in his voice. She smiled a guilty smile, because even though their relationship was strained, his desire to protect her was always very evident.

"Overall, yes," she said, "I'm just kind of stuck on the BW Parkway."

"What?" She could hear the panic in his voice. "What happened? Are you ok?" She heard the set of keys he picked up. Without hesitation or explanation, he was on his way to pick her up. That made her feel even guiltier

"I'm fine Shawn. My tire was punctured last week when I went over a curb, and it just went flat on my way back from a meeting."

"Where exactly are you? Are you pulled over?"

Alonna described where she was. "I'm fine. I'm on the shoulder, so I'm not in traffic."

"Ok, that's good. I'm on my way." With that Alonna heard the car start before he hung up the phone.

A tear escaped her eye. She felt the guilt and embarrassment at her behavior in the past few weeks. She had treated him so badly, and amazingly he was once again bending over backwards to take care of her.

****

Within thirty minutes of giving Shawn directions, his car pulled up behind her on the busy parkway. Even dressed in sweatpants and a worn t-shirt, the man was fine. In the two months since they broke up, she could tell he had been going to the gym more. Alonna shook her head. Not confronting her thoughts was what got her in trouble in the first place.

"Thank you so much for coming." She ran over to him.

"No problem" Shawn responded. His gaze seemed to linger on her reminding her of how good things used to be.

"Let's see what we have here," he said as he inspected the flat tire. Within minutes he retrieved his tools from his vehicle and set to work on putting a spare tire on her car. The anxiety that previously weighed on her heart quickly disappeared as Alonna watched him work with fervor. There was no denying that Shawn Williams was one of God's physically finest creations. Twenty minutes later Alonna had a replacement tire on her car, ready to go home. She reached over to hug Shawn, who moved away slightly.

"Thank you so much."

"No problem," he responded as he picked up his tools to put back in his car.

"Can I buy you lunch or something?" Alonna asked walking behind him. "Please? Just to say thank you."

"That's not necessary," Shawn responded coldly. "Be safe, please."

Alonna could hear the hurt in his voice, which hurt her in turn.

She reached for his hand, "please let me buy you lunch, or at least a soda. You didn't have to drop what you were doing to come help me."

"That's what people do when they care about someone."

His words were cold. Even his voice sounded unnatural talking to her like that. It pained her to hear the sarcasm in his voice. She swallowed her pride and fought the urge to respond with a sarcastic remark of her own.

"Shawn, you are right. I have not been the kindest or most gracious person," Alonna stated, "I am sorry. Could we please talk about this over lunch?"

Shawn paused, staring at her as if contemplating an appropriate   response.

"Look," he said, "I only want to be around people who appreciate me, Alonna. I do not need to be around people who see me as a project, or who will blame me every time something goes wrong, without taking responsibility for their actions. I think I am a pretty decent human being, and believe it or not, there are actually people who like me for me."

His words stung.

Alonna put her head down. "You are right. I deserve that."

Before she could finish her sentence, Shawn interrupted her. "And look, just because I don't see things your way, does not mean that I do not have feelings."

Alonna did not respond.

"You tried to force me to come to church, but maybe you're looking for some things there too?"

Alonna knew it was a rhetorical question, but she responded anyway.

"You are right, Shawn. Can we at least go in the car and talk about this? I feel crazy standing here talking about this."

"We can't stay here and talk, but why don't you drive behind me? I have a few minutes to spare. Rock Creek Park is only a few miles from here. We can talk there."

Alonna happily obliged.

Ten minutes later, Alonna pulled up behind him. When they arrived at the park, she knew there was something that he needed to know. The entire ride over she'd thought about how to best tell him her secret. She'd never told anyone, and although today was as good a day as any, she wondered if she was making the right decision.

What if he ran away, or called her nasty names? What if he told everyone she knew about what a hypocrite she was?

She closed her car door and walked to fall in step with him. With each step, her legs seemed to grow weaker. From the way he was walking, had it not been his idea, she would have thought he did not want to be there.

"Make sure you get that tire taken care of as soon as possible," was all he said as she finally caught up and sat down on the park bench next to him.

Alonna pretended not to hear him.

"Shawn, the reason I have been behaving like this is because I have trust issues," she went straight to the point. If she was going to tell him, it was better she say it quickly before she changed her mind. For the next fifteen minutes she went on and explained how her relationship with Ray affected her, and how she still struggled with guilt and low self-esteem because of her decisions during that time. Shawn was completely silent, and Alonna took that as permission to continue talking.

She looked up only occasionally to gauge whether he was still sitting there listening. She'd half-expected that he had ran out after hearing most of the gory details. She'd confessed most of the details of how her relationship with Ray went from one of complete bliss to disaster overnight, and how she endured the verbal abuse, mostly because her self-esteem had been so damaged by that point. She talked about the humiliation of calling of the engagement after walking in on Ray with another woman, and the lack of support from her father because he'd assumed she'd driven him away. By this time she was already in tears at having to relive the last three years all over again. While it was cathartic to talk about it with someone, for Alonna it also felt like someone was ripping off the bandage of an old wound.

When she couldn't avoid saying it anymore, she confessed to the details of the operation. Shawn hadn't asked. In fact, he'd barely spoke since she started talking, but she knew that her story was incomplete without talking about the one decision that still haunted her. The dark halls, the cold feel of the instruments, and the shameful looks of the other women in the waiting area, she talked about it all. She spared no detail, because at this point, there was no going back.

Alonna could recall the looks of the other women. That was the most startling part of the whole experience. She'd expected to see a room full of scared teenage girls. Instead she saw a mixture of young girls with adult boyfriends or overbearing mothers, well-groomed professional women who appeared undisturbed by the whole process, and a few young adults with looks of concerned etched on their faces.

When she could not talk anymore, Alonna breathed a sigh of relief and buried her face in her hand. The weight of the baggage had finally been released, but embarrassment was too much to bear, and she did not want to face Shawn.

She'd just made the biggest confession of her life, and all she could think about was Shawn's response. Would he curse her, laugh at her or expose her? Alonna became lost in her own thoughts. She could not stand the thought of losing him, but she would understand if he never wanted to see her again.

She was startled by the hand that was now enclosing hers. She looked over at Shawn, whose eyes were closed as if deep in thought. His lips remained still, and for the seemingly unending moments that passed his hand never left hers. In all of the scenarios that she had conjured in her mind, this was not the response she expected.

His expression was serene. He was non-judgmental, even supportive. As if she wasn't already feeling this way, she was now certain that she loved him. She knew that she had given him news that would cause many to run away from the stigma attached to it. She could not understand how he could respond like that, especially after what she did to him a few weeks back. As if he could feel her eyes on him, Shawn intertwined their fingers together as a show of solidarity. Alonna remained speechless and simply allowed the tears to flow. She'd finally done it. She no longer carried the weight of her past and what she had done. Perhaps now the cries that she heard at night would cease.

Shawn was the first to speak.

"Alonna, I understand how you feel, but not every man will treat you the way that idiot treated you." He was now facing her.

"I wish I could make all the pain go away. If I could, I would." He continued as his hands balled up.

"If I knew where that coward was right now, I would gladly give him a dose of his own medicine, and make him pay for being a coward and making you go through that alone."

Alonna cried and buried her head in his chest. Shawn stroked her hair as the two rocked back and forth. After a few seconds, he managed to say, "Thank you for telling me."

Alonna nodded in silence.

He continued, "I can imagine the fear and the anxiety of not wanting to tell anyone."

Alonna continued nodding.

Shawn leaned back and held Alonna's face in his hands. Seeing her so distraught made him forget how upset he'd been with her. "I know this was hard for you to tell me, and the only thing I have to say is please let me be there for you," he pleaded

With tears filling her eyes, Alonna shook her head.

"You don't have to make a decision now, but I would still like to be there for you. I won't lie to you. I accept you with mistakes and all, and nothing will change that."

His eyes and words both seemed sincere, but Alonna thought back to a recent conversation they'd had about marriage and children. The possibility of not being able to have children taunted her daily. Although a doctor never confirmed it, the fear laid dormant. She feared that as a punishment for what she'd done, perhaps God would close up any likelihood of her having children. Although Shawn did not say that, Alonna could not help but think that he was probably considering the same thing. She knew he cared too much to say anything out loud.

"I wish I could have protected you." Shawn gently turned her face to face his.

"All I want to do, Alonna, is protect you. I don't hold your past against you. Please let me do that."

Alonna rested her head on his shoulder. "But I'm damaged goods now. If you have a chance to be with someone who is not, you should take it."

Alonna was not just saying these words, but she'd woken up to this truth everyday for the past three years. She knew of no other reality. She'd heard the voices clearly—if she couldn't have children, it was because that's what she deserved.

"The scars from what I've done haunt me daily. The way I treated you a few weeks back is evidence of that. I feel like a ticking time bomb that may go off at any time."

Shawn leaned down slightly and kissed her forehead.

"I have met many women Alonna, and I have yet to meet one with more class, confidence, intelligence, and beauty than you. If our mistakes determine our worth, then we are all worthless. As a Christian you should know that!" he exclaimed.

She looked up at him, and for the first time in over an hour she cracked a smile. She nudged him playfully. "So now you're a pastor?"

"You never know." Shawn smiled back playfully.

Alonna said a silent prayer and marveled at his insight. She still struggled with balancing her mistakes with her self-worth. Although she knew from all her years in church and bible study that they were quite separate issues. She knew conceptually that God's grace for the believer covered her sins, and that He was not vengeful. The problem was moving beyond conceptual belief so that it resonated in her heart.

She wanted to ask him what all of it meant for their relationship, but she was not sure she knew the answer herself. She'd learned the price of compromise, and she did not want to go back there. For now, she was content with knowing he knew her completely, and did not despise her.

Chapter 19

There was a slight knock on the door. The week after a long weekend always seemed to go by slowly. The price of a four-day work week was having a make up all the missed work from taking off to get her car inspected. She was irritated, and the deadline for a grant that the center desperately needed was fast approaching. She'd learned early on that in the nature of her work, a closed door policy was just not a luxury she could afford.

"Come in," she said, trying her best to mask her irritation.

The door opened slowly, and she saw Renee. Almost instantly, Alonna knew that whatever was causing Renee to interrupt her work was serious.

"Hi lady, what's up?" Alonna put her pen off and took off her reading glasses.

"Hi, Ms. Alonna."

Alonna noticed that the young girl could barely look up as she spoke to her. From the first day she met her,

Renee had been anything but coy. Alonna walked over and gently helped Renee to the seat.

"What's going on Renee? Is everything ok?"

She could barely finish her question before Renee began to cry. Renee's hands covered her face as she shook her head slowly. Alonna heard the young girl whisper "no" several times. She went around her desk for the box of Kleenex. She could hear Renee muttering, "I can't believe this is happening to me."

Alonna got the tissues and sat down in the chair next to Renee. "Honey, talk to me. What's going on? Whatever it is, we can fix it," she said as assuredly as she could.

For the first time since entering the room, Renee made eye contact as she looked up at Alonna. "Miss Alonna, this can't be fixed," she said softly.

Renee continued, "I did everything right. The one time I make a mistake, and my whole life gets screwed up."

Alonna reached for Renee, but Renee flinched and got up to walk away.

"I knew I wasn't gon' be anything. Everybody always told me that I ain't gon' be nobody, and now it's true."

Alonna reached for the girl again.

"Honey, I'm confused. Slow down, and explain to me what's going on."

With tears in her eyes, Renee looked up at Alonna. "Miss Alonna, I'm so ashamed. I don't even want to tell you."

As a show of support, Alonna grabbed Renee's hand and walked her back over to the chairs. "You don't ever have to be ashamed to tell me anything." Alonna quoted a line from a Ledell song, in hopes that it would cause Renee to loosen up.

She continued to hold on to the girl's hand. Just days earlier, Alonna had observed Renee running around and talking with the other girls in the group. Alonna wondered what could have changed so drastically in a matter of days to cause her to react like this.

Alonna was startled out of her thoughts as she heard Renee ask "Ms. Alonna, do you hate me now? I know I disappointed you, and I am so sorry."

"I don't understand sweetie. What are you so sorry about?"

Averting her eyes away, Renee softly responded, "I'm pregnant."

Alonna could hardly believe her ears. She hoped that that her face did not reflect her surprise at the news. The easiest way to turn a teenager, or anyone for that matter, off was to make them feel judged and condemned. In an effort to hide her initial reaction, Alonna reached for Renee and hugged the young girl. When did this happen, she wondered to herself. To the best of her knowledge, Renee was an active girl, who did not have time to engage in risky behavior. Between her obligations for school, The Journey House, college applications and her part-time job, it would seem she would not have time for anything else.

"When did you find out?" Alonna asked evenly, trying her best to hide her surprise.

"This morning. I had been throwing up for the last two weeks, and my momma made me take a test this morning. Ms. Alonna, I can't even show my face at my house anymore. Everyone was counting on me to be different."

133

Alonna tried her best to remain the calm adult. She had been there and she knew that this was a life altering situation, but the last thing she needed was for Renee to panic.

"Renee, believe me when I tell you that there are worse things in life. Trust me." Alonna wished that she could share her story with Renee, but she'd hid the details well for so long, and to divulge the information to a teenage girl, would risk her best kept secret being publicized to the world.

Renee looked up at Alonna angrily. "What can be worse like this? How am I going to go to college?"

Alonna was at a loss for words.

"Ms. Alonna, I don't mean no disrespect, but you are just not going to understand. My momma had me when she was 16. Her momma had her when she was 15. My sister, at least, waited until she was 18. Now here I am, at 17, doing the same thing they all did."

Renee was no longer making an attempt to cover her face or wipe her tears. Alonna felt her pain. They were exactly the same, but unlike her, Renee actually had the courage to speak up about what she was going through.

"What are you going to do?" Was all Alonna could ask.

Renee looked up, but did not speak. Alonna was familiar with the confusion and sadness in her eyes. She was the same just years ago.

"I can't keep this baby," Renee finally managed after a few minutes. She put her head down.

"Did you talk to your mom about this?" Alonna asked quietly. Now was not the time for a lecture or a sermon.

"It's her idea," Renee explained in between sobs.

"Ms. Alonna, I'm scared. I don't want to, but I have to. The father is a deadbeat. He was a mistake. My whole life is a mistake. I cannot bring a child into this world who's not gon' have a father."

Before Renee said that, Alonna had not even thought about that part. She wondered if the father could be any of the boys that also frequented The Journey House. For the sake of the center's critics, she hoped not.

Snapped out of her thoughts, she listened as Renee described a childhood that involved her single mother trying to keep a roof over their head, the multiple evictions from apartments that they could not afford, and being teased by other children because her family was on public assistance.

Alonna felt for the young girl, but she also knew that pregnancy did not have to mean the end of her life. Alonna wondered if anything she could say would even make much of a difference, especially if things were as bad as Renee was describing them. She did not want to ask Renee when she was so upset, but perhaps if she knew who the father was, she could offer support to both of them.

"Listen, let me tell you something. I'm going to share something that very few people know about me. Not even my best friends know."

Renee looked up at Alonna desperate to hear something that would make her situation better. Before Alonna could stop herself, she found herself divulging the secret that, prior to telling Shawn, she swore she would take to her grave.

When Alonna was finished talking, both she and Renee were crying. With mixed emotions, Alonna reached over and hugged the girl. The comfort of releasing the burden along with the fear of the unknown in Renee's eyes mirrored the thoughts that Alonna was thinking.

Renee cried as she mourned the future that she'd envisioned for herself, and Alonna cried as she mourned the past that she would never be able to change.

****

Alonna stared at the pink notebook next to her bed. It had been a while, but she knew that this was the perfect time to pick up the habit she started when she was just eleven years old. Back then her heartbreaks included not getting the latest toys for Christmas, or being punished for getting a bad grade in school. The times had changed. When she was packing her things to move back to Virginia, she'd found the pink notebook that carefully held all of her most precious thoughts and best-kept secrets. It had been in a box next to the dozens of other notebooks that held similar secrets and chronicled her most intimate moments from her teenage years to adulthood. With little else to do with all of the emotions that were weighing her down, she picked up a pen. She had learned a few years back that journaling, no matter how old one is, is one of the healthiest coping strategies for stress. For her it had always been about introspection and self-evaluation. Today she just needed the little notebook to be the listening ear that she felt no one else could be for her at the moment.

Thirty minutes later, Alonna closed her journal. She'd written about the pain of Renee's decision. Despite all of her efforts to convince the girl otherwise, Renee was insistent that terminating her pregnancy was her only option. Alonna also wrote about Shawn. It had been four months since they separated, and each passing day seemed to confirm that the decision to separate was a permanent decision. While she knew the decision was best, it hurt nonetheless. She took one more Tylenol.

She could hear her mother's voice. *Don't take so many pills honey. Those don't really solve the problem, only prayer does.*

Alonna had tried both. She'd had many nights when all she could do was lay prostrate by her bed and cry out to God. She'd also tried the medicinal approach, but the headaches would not subside. Between trying to decide on the next steps in her relationship with Shawn, grieving for Renee and the fact that innocence had forever been lost, and her deadline for work that was quickly approaching, Alonna was exhausted.

When she first moved back to Virginia, Alonna had given herself one year to have The Journey House up and running. Thanks to the generous contributions from Pastor Paul, in a matter of months the center was well on its way there. However, desperate financial needs threatened to end all she'd worked hard for. The fact that she'd given up a lucrative position, led to many questionable looks and a barrage of questions from loved ones and associates who had reason to question her judgment. For the most part, Alonna had remained steadfast. She had heard clearly from God, and that was all the support she needed.

In the few weeks that The Journey House had become fully operational, Alonna grew to understand that it was like a child, created perfectly for her. She loved the teens, the staff and volunteers, and the work she did brought her great satisfaction. Now, her own story was coming full circle with one of her youth. With Renee, all she could do was pray that God would keep her from making the same mistakes she'd made. For most things,

Alonna could think of a solution. However, despite her efforts, some of the challenges would be without solutions this time.

Alonna reached for the bottle of pain relievers on her bedside. Then she realized she had taken three pills in the last three hours, and decided against it. She pulled up her covers and decided that perhaps she could sleep her problems away.

Chapter 20

Alonna turned up the music as Ledell's latest song "picture perfect" came on her Pandora radio station. Ever since she found out about Ledell from Grace and Renee, she couldn't stop listening to the talented singer's album. Alonna found that she could relate to all of her songs, which covered topics from beauty, love, consciousness, and faith—all things that resonated with her. Her latest song about freedom was quickly becoming Alonna's favorite.

She was not ashamed to be singing out loud by herself in the car. A few times she caught the mocking glances of drivers in other cars, but Alonna continued to sing and drive in complete bliss. With the kind of day she was having, she deserved a moment to sing out loud—even if it was just to herself.

The day had started off with a completely random turn of events. Shortly after she woke up in the morning, she'd received a phone call from Ari. In over 10 years that she'd known her friend, she'd never heard such distress in her voice. Ari explained how the previous night she got home around 11pm, and called Kyle because she was worried and had not heard from him for much of the day.

Even before Ari got to the end of the story, she knew where it was heading. She had been in similar situations a few too many times. Alonna thought about how Kyle did not come across as that type, but then again, the older she got, the more she realized that there was no such thing as a type.

Ari explained that between 11pm and 11:30pm she called and texted Kyle several times, but received no answer. Although it was no laughing matter, Alonna chuckled at the fact that by 11:30pm her usually reserved friend had driven to his house and staked out to see if anyone was home. When she realized by midnight that her boyfriend was not home, she tried his cell phone again only for him to call and say that he was still at the office completing a project. Ari went on to explain how her night ended with her going back to his home thirty minutes later, to discover that Kyle was still not home. This time she stated she was done for good, because at 12:30am, she left her engagement ring, wrapped in a plastic bag, on his front porch.

Ari described that within the first few months of their relationship, they had mastered a routine—part of their groove as a couple was that each kept the other abreast of the other's dealings during the day. Ari knew that while she was at work from 9am to 5pm, Kyle was typically at work and in meetings at that same time. Whenever there were variations in their daily schedule, one would always let the other know. She always knew those appointments and activities. Alonna could hear Ari crying on the phone as she explained that she has long believed that Kyle was cheating on her. The events of the day were enough to confirm what she already believed.

While she was sad that her friend had given an undeserving man too many wonderful years of her life, she admired her decision to do what she herself was incapable of doing when she was in a similar situation.

Alonna thought of her own relationship with Shawn. While they were together, she'd never doubted his fidelity. However, she could never really let her guard down, because the last thing she needed was to have another man cheat on her, especially since she had been fighting so hard to escape the "all men are dogs" syndrome.

As they continued talking, Alonna listened as Ari expressed disappointment in herself for having missed what should have been obvious to her. Ari described the changes in Kyle's attitude, and explained that he'd stopped paying attention to her as he did before. One thing Alonna had learned early on in her relationship with Ray is that withdrawal is usually the first sign that something or someone else had caught a man's attention. She remembered her naïveté as she believed that maybe he could be one of the good ones who really practiced what he preached. Instead, she let the issues go unaddressed as their communication had gone from texting and calling several times a day, to once a day—right before one person went to bed. She'd ignored the distance and had chosen to discard her suspicions because she feared the day she would receive confirmation. The deadliest mistake she ever made in her life was to ignore those signs until it was too late.

As she listened to Ari, she did not bring up her own situation, because it was Ari's time to vent, to release, to begin the healing process. As they ended their conversation, Alonna assured Ari that while the mourning would hurt, she would be ok. Ari had been a rock for her during her breakup with Ray, and now it was her turn to be there for her friend.

Alonna thought about where she was emotionally three years ago, and how what seemed like the worst time of her life, had turned into a period that produced much strength in her, and rekindled her faith in herself. After she'd gotten off the phone with Ari, Alonna picked up her gym bag and headed to the gym. It was definitely a good time to let off some steam.

Now, as she sat in the car, listening to the latest Ledell song, she was singing in optimism not just in celebration of her new journey, but what she knew would be Ari's journey as well. Although her friend was hurting, it was better that she shed any deadweight now, than after she invested any more of herself in someone that did not deserve her.

Alonna pulled into one of the few empty spaces at the gym, but stayed in the car to hear the end of a song that spoke about freedom and second chances.

Alonna had a new lease on life. The Journey House was progressing just fine, she'd received some peace about her relationship with Shawn, and she had begun seeing a difference in her health goals. Alonna smiled as she looked down at her legs. So far she had lost twelve pounds, and was surely not going to stop there. She thought to herself, "twelve down, and thirteen to go." There was always thirteen more to go, she laughed to herself.

****

Alonna found herself getting more and more excited about her plans for the night. Earlier in the week, she, Nicole and Ari decided that they would go on a mini-vacation for the three-day holiday weekend. She could not remember the last time they had an old-school sleepover.

Perhaps it was in college, when their biggest worries included what to wear on a date with a random guy from campus, or how to drop twenty pounds in two weeks to fit into a dress for homecoming. Alonna missed those days, and she planned on reliving them to the fullest tonight.

They'd made plans to rent a hotel room in Ocean City, Maryland—a two-hour drive from DC. They'd be far enough to escape the traffic and noise of the city, but close enough that they did not have to rush back to resume life as they knew it.

She was also glad to get away because she was starting to miss Shawn more and more. With Ari's recent enrollment in the single's club, their mini-retreat was coming at a perfect time. She shook her head as she quietly wondered how she had even gotten to this point. She, Alonna "Ms. Independent" Jones, was actually missing a man. Not just any man, a man she practically chased away and laughed at in the process. She was thankful to get her mind off all that drama. She packed her overnight clothes, an extra outfit, the girls' favorite movie *Hitched*, and the brownies and cookies she'd made for the night.

Two hours later, Alonna pulled into the hotel parking lot. She knew that just about every hotel would be booked tonight by students who were also taking advantage of the three-day weekend as an opportunity to do things that some would later regret. She quietly thanked God for the growth she had experienced in recent years. Those days were well past her.

Alonna picked up her overnight bag and headed toward the hotel. She noticed that Nicole and Ari were already in there because the first thing she saw in the parking lot was Ari's bright green Volkswagen Beatle. The car was a perfect reflection of her personality. She and

Nicole must have carpooled because Alonna did not see Nicole's car there.

Minutes after checking in, Ari was opening the door for her, already dressed in her pajamas as if it weren't only 6pm in the evening.

"Well, hello to you too. There are too many things wrong with this picture," Alonna said laughing as she looked at Ari up and down

"Don't be jealous," Ari joked as she gave her friend a hug.

"Come on in, and stop laughing at me," Ari said closing the door behind her.

Alonna walked by her and put her things on the floor.

"You know why I'm laughing, right?" Alonna asked still laughing.

"Of course she knows," Nicole jumped in from the suite kitchenette. "It's because it is as confusing to you as it is to me, why a woman pushing thirty years of age is still wearing cartoon pajamas to sleep, and at 6pm at that," Nicole teased.

"Oh hush" Ari turned toward her and shrugged, "I just wanted to be comfortable, and these are what I called 'old faithful' when it comes to comfort."

Alonna busted out laughing. Already, the night was starting well. She could count on Ari's antics and Nicole's bluntness to keep her entertained all night.

The three ladies wasted no time delving into the night's activities. They planned to cook dinner together, and then watch movies to their heart's content. Alonna knew well that neither of these activities would be without a good dose of chatter and laughter.

An hour later, the three sat down to a meal of lasagna, steamed broccoli, and Ari's famous cornbread to go along with the deserts that Alonna volunteered to bake. As she sat down to dinner, Alonna made a mental note to do an extra thirty minutes at the gym on Monday.

Nicole, with her usual bluntness, was the first to start the evening with the prying questions. "So, how are things with Mr. ex-loverboy?"

Determined not to continue her pity party from earlier in the day, Alonna answered in a sober and even voice.

"I think he's fine. I don't know what he's doing, and frankly, I don't care." Even she didn't buy into the bravado in her voice. She said it in hopes of convincing herself. The reality was that she did care, but several weeks had passed since her last conversation with him. Besides the occasional text messages from Shawn to check in on her, neither had taken any real steps toward reconciling the relationship. Perhaps it was better that way, Alonna had decided.

Alonna heard Ari snicker.

"What's so funny?" she asked.

"Nothing, just this game of "pretend" that you're playing."

Alonna narrowed her eyes at her. "What does that mean" Alonna asked.

This time it was Nicole's turn to blow her cover. "It means you can drop the act, Loni," She said as gently as she could.

"Everyone here already knows how much you care about little Shawn." She laughed.

Alonna rolled her eyes. "First of all, can we please not refer to him as little Shawn? He's bigger than both of us

145

put together. Second of all, I do care, but I can't waste all my time worried about some man that I am not meant to be with."

"Well, wait a minute" Ari answered. "What makes you so sure that you are not supposed to be with him?" Ari had been asking herself that question lately, and a part of her was hoping Alonna's answer would help shed some insight into her situation.

"And what makes you feel like caring about someone and missing them is a waste of time?" Nicole added.

"I mean the differences between us are clear. He's not spiritually where I would need a man to be for me, and on top of it all, he's a mechanic, so naturally his friends and interests are different from mine." Alonna paused, "and in case you forgot, he's got the tall and handsome part down, but not the dark part. You both are the first to remind me of that."

Ignoring Alonna's jab at her previous statements, Nicole asked, "so, who died and made you God to predetermine someone's spiritual journey?"

The question stung, but Alonna knew her friend did not mean any harm.

"I understand that concern totally, Loni," Ari rushed to Alonna's defense.

"All I can say is continue to pray. From what I understand about Shawn, right now he's hurt, and rightfully so. Because we know that as children of God there are no such things as coincidences, be open to how the Lord will lead you. Not every man that says he's a man of God, really is. And not every man that is struggling is a lost cause."

Alonna could hear a hint of sadness as Ari said the last part. She knew immediately that she was referring to Kyle.

"So, how's that joker doing anyway?" Nicole asked.

"What are you talking about" asked Ari defensively.

"The one who can't keep his stuff in his pocket." Nicole giggled and Alonna was tempted to join in with her, but thought better of it when she saw the hurt look on Ari's face.

"That joker is someone that I really care about, and I am upset with myself for that." Ari responded with an edge in her voice.

There were times when Nicole's brashness and insensitivity did more harm than good. Alonna had learned how to accept it, but sometimes it was a bit much for Ari to handle.

Alonna empathized with her friend, "I'm sorry, Ari. I know it's hard now, but it gets easier. Kyle had all of us fooled. You are a great woman, and you are going to make a true man of God a great wife someday."

"Thanks Loni, but I've wasted so much time that I will never get back."

Ari's self-esteem had been damaged right along with her relationship with Kyle. This, too, was familiar to Alonna.

"Why do we need to have these pity parties?" Nicole interjected. "I came here to celebrate, not cry all night."

"Why do you have to be so cynical?" Ari burst out.

"We get it, you are the big executive. You are too busy to even have a man. That's not our fault. If you won't allow yourself to feel, can you please give us mere humans the time to do so?"

Alonna reached over to calm Ari down. She knew it was only a matter of time before Ari burst. Of the three, Nicole was the harshest, and Ari was the most sensitive. She managed to remain even-keeled, which served their relationship well.

"Ladies, calm down." Alonna said. "We are all going through a lot right now. Remember, that is the point of getting away."

Things were quickly becoming heated, and Alonna did not like it. In over ten years of being friends, they'd gotten into arguments before, but now was the time they needed each other.

"So, why don't you tell me how you really feel," Nicole said derisively. "'You think you know, but you have no idea."

Alonna could hear the frustration in Nicole's voice. Ari looked up at Nicole with a look of confusion. Alonna, too, was confused about what Nicole could possibly be referring to.

"I am tired of being alone." Nicole's finally said as she buried her head in her hands.

"I have the perfect house, an amazing job, great friends, everyone knows me, but at the end of the day, I am so lonely." Alonna was now rushing over to Nicole's side. Ari remained where she was. She was still a little upset at Nicole's earlier statements.

Nicole looked up at them, and for the first time in years, Alonna saw tears in her eyes. She was always the strong one.

"For my 30th birthday, you know what my crazy mother got me?"

Alonna remembered the Vera Wang wedding dress that Nicole had shown her from her mother. The three had had a good laugh at what they thought was a practical joke.

As if reading her mind, Nicole responded, "Nicely tucked inside the dress, was a book, *How to Get a Man Before Your Eggs Dry up.*"

Alonna stifled the laugh that was threatening to escape from her mouth. Seconds later she heard Ari. She had been unsuccessful in stifling hers. Seconds after that Alonna heard Nicole join in. She loved her friends for that reason. No matter the situation, most times they were able to find some kind of humor in it.

Then with all seriousness, Nicole explained how hurt she'd been by the gift. Alonna knew that since they were in college, Alonna's mother tended to be a practical joker. Whenever she got together with the girls, she'd made them laugh for hours.

In typical form, in a matter of hours, they'd gone from crying and laughing together, to being upset and challenging each other.

The night superseded all of Alonna's expectations, and even she was surprised when she looked over at the clock to discover that it was 2AM before she started to feel sleepy.

"You guys know I love you, but if I don't go to sleep, it's going to be bad for everyone involved tomorrow."

"You mean today," said Ari.

Alonna smiled at Ari's attempt to be witty, "sure."

Alonna straightened her bed and realized that she'd spent almost 6 hours without missing or worrying about Shawn. That was a record these days.

Chapter 21

Alonna knew that no matter how long she prolonged it, she had to extend the olive branch today. During an earlier conversation with her mother, Alonna had learned that unbeknownst to her, her father had used up half of their life's savings to invest in a friend's business. It was only after a conversation with Grace about college prompted her to check their account, that Delores discovered the large sum of money that was missing.

Alonna was livid at the news. His recklessness had gone beyond tolerance, because not only had he ruined their family and destroyed her mother's self-esteem in the process, but now he was messing with Grace. It took what little bit of self-control Alonna had to keep from telling him how little respect she had for him. She'd been angrier than she'd ever been before, and it was not until she heard a sermon from T.D. Jakes, that she thought about extending any olive branch. She was not sure why she was doing it, but today was probably as good a day as any to do so because today was his birthday. Given her renewed commitment to God, she knew that she could not let the day go by without at least wishing him a happy birthday, even if she did not get him a gift.

Sometimes, forgiveness is more for you than the other person. Those were the words spoken by Pastor Paul on Sunday, which served as further confirmation for what she needed to do.

After three rings, her father picked up the phone. "Hello?"

"Hi dad," Alonna responded. She hoped that her voice did not reflect the sense of obligation she felt. She knew it was a sad day when she was calling her own father more out of obligation than desire.

"How are you, baby girl?"

"I'm fine. How are you? Happy Birthday."

"I'm fine," her father responded. "I was wondering if you were going to call your ol' dad."

It was his attempt at a joke.

"It's been a long day, and I was just busy with work."

"Oh, ok. That's good to hear, baby girl. How is the business?"

Alonna could hear the feigned excitement in her father's voice. She had learned early on that there were two things that her father was good at: deflecting issues off himself, and being vulnerable with his family. She had spent many nights praying that the man she married would not possess those same attributes. As much as she loved her mother, she doubted that she could stay in a relationship like her parents.

"Everything is great. Things are running very smoothly." Her response was short and sweet—the usual way she responded to him. It really was a shame that at her age the damage done in their relationship seemed irreversible.

"Listen dad, I have to run," Alonna lied. "I have a lot of work to get done, but I just called to wish you a happy birthday."

The olive branch was short, but at least she made an attempt by calling him.

There was a short pause. Even over the phone, the tension could be cut with a knife. Seconds later, the question came ringing out.

"Why did it take you so long to come back home, baby?" Her father sounded sincere, but he and Alonna had never been one for sentimentality.

"I'm sorry?" Alonna had to be sure she heard the question correctly.

"Listen, baby girl, I know that our relationship has not been the best. There are so many things that I wish I could do over. One of those things is to undo the damage that caused you to move so far from home. I have always wondered if there was something I did that made you stay away for so long."

Alonna had never considered the question before. The fact was that she'd moved because she was chasing a dream. She could not say for certain that their volatile relationship had nothing to do with it, but it was hard to explain tunnel vision to most people.

"Anyway, thanks for calling me. We'll talk soon."

Her father had misunderstood her silence.

"Dad," Alonna breathed a long sigh. If stubborn Willie Jones could extend his own olive branch, the least she could do was accept it.

"You had nothing to do with that decision." Technically, she wasn't lying. "You and momma raised me to be independent and to fend for myself. At the time, all I really wanted was to be able to make a name for myself."

"I understand, baby girl." She could tell that her dad was disappointed with her response.

"The truth is," she continued, "I wish we could have had a better relationship, but my leaving was not so much about leaving your home, as it was about trying to create a new home for myself."

"What do you mean?" her dad asked.

Alonna could no longer hold the thoughts to herself. "Daddy, you were sometimes downright cruel. I remember talking to momma after the cancer scare and being upset and panicked, because I knew that if anything happened to her, you may not take care of me or Grace."

Her father tried to interrupt, but now she was on a roll.

"I didn't so much care about myself, because I was already an adult, but all I could think about was little Grace. Daddy, you were selfish. Most times it seemed you loved the bottle more than your own family."

She hadn't meant for the words to come out the way they did, but she couldn't stop herself. For the first time in her life, she was given the opportunity to release the thoughts and disappointment that he never seemed to care about.

"I'm sorry you felt that way, Alonna." She could hear the hurt in his voice. "Baby, I wish I could explain to you the type of demons I was fighting."

There was a long pause. Alonna knew he was referring to his battle with alcoholism, but she was disappointed that their family had not been enough motivation for him to fight his so-called demons.

"I didn't just feel that way back then. Sometimes, I still feel that way." Alonna tried her best to stop the tears, but to no avail. "Me leaving Arlington was my effort to make a home for myself. To redesign life as I imagined it should be, because I never really left our home was really a home. If momma had died, I wanted to create a safe and comfortable space for me and Grace. Then it would not matter if you decided to blow sick thousand dollars, or if you were never around when we were sick." Alonna listed some of her father's transgressions.

"Home is supposed to be where you feel the safest daddy, but for me, most times I associated it with anger, hurt, and downright cruelty." If her mother was not going to speak up for herself, Alonna would do it for her. The sudden boldness felt good.

It was only after she'd gotten all of her feelings out, that she heard her father sobbing. She was nearly thirty, and she could only remember two times that she'd seen or heard her father cry. Alonna fought to suppress the guilt that was rising up in her. Perhaps she had been too harsh, but she had not called with the intention of giving her own father a verbal lashing, but he'd started the conversation.

She heard her dad clear his throat. "Alonna, I am very sorry that you feel that way. I wish I knew you felt this strongly earlier. Perhaps things would have been different."

Alonna thought about all of the major decisions she'd made in recent years. Perhaps if she'd have a father that was more concerned about his daughter than his friends, she would not have promised to marry a heartless man. Perhaps she would have felt safe enough to come home after the nights of crying, if he'd called her just to tell her that he loved her. Thinking about all the perhaps wouldn't do any good now—they were just memories and mysteries.

Just the Sunday before, Pastor Paul had preached about coming face to face with the opportunity to forgive.

Alonna thought about how ironic it was that she was having this conversation with her father. If ever she had a moment to come face to face with the opportunity to forgive, this was it. She knew that this was the closest she'd ever come to an apology from her father, and the decision was hers to decide whether or not to forgive. It was likely that if she waited for a formal apology in which he listed all the wrong he'd done to their family, she may never get one.

In his typical manner, her father deflected all that happened and cited his upbringing and demands of work for why things were the way they were. She and her father talked for a few minutes longer, but before Alonna hung up the phone, Willie Jones made one more confession.

"For what it's worth, baby girl, I haven't touched a drink in eleven months."

The tears began to flow. She spent most of her teenage years, hoping to hear those words.

"I'm proud of you, daddy."

She sincerely meant that. At twenty-nine, she knew what it meant to battle demons and lose, and she had an appreciation for each time she could successfully walk away from something that once held her hostage.

"Thank you baby girl," was all her father said as they got off the phone.

For the first time in a long time, that was enough for Alonna. She'd wanted to talk to her dad and demand that he treat her mother better. Something told her this was not the right conversation for that. All she could do was pray that grace would continue to take its course. In her heart she knew the work had already begun, because, if he was telling truth, then only a miracle could separate her father from the bottle for eleven months.

Chapter 22

Alonna had learned one important thing—God's timing was not her own, and His was always better. After the long and trying weeks, she'd finally received the breakthrough that she'd been praying for. Alonna meditated on that as she pulled into The Journey House.

Just earlier that morning, she'd received the news that The Journey House would be receiving the $20,000 grant she applied for. She had spent endless nights writing the grant, and could not have been happier.

"Good morning Alonna," Melody, the new administrative assistant, happily sang.

"How are you this morning, Melody?" asked Alonna with a failed attempt at matching the other's cheerfulness.

She knew she'd made a great decision in hiring Melody as the new administrative assistant. For someone who had been through a lot herself as a troubled youth, her joy was always overflowing. Now that they were getting ready to move into their own building, she was confident that she would get adequate help in the transition.

"I'm fine. I can't complain." Melody flashed her famous smile. "Justin got accepted to Georgetown!" she exclaimed. "I just wanted to say thank you, because it would not have happened without you."

Melody was referring to Alonna's call to the Associate Dean of the university on Justin's behalf. Melody was a single mother who tried her best in raising Justin. When the teen first came to the program, he was considered bright but troubled. He'd gotten involved with some local thugs, and despite his high scores on aptitude tests, he'd decided that school was just not for him. That was eight months ago and right before his senior year in high school. Alonna had worked closely with the mentors in the program to redirect Justin back to the right path. Thankfully, he'd done enough good work and earned good grades in his first two years of high school that he would be able to graduate on time.

At 6'4, Alonna had learned that his tough demeanor was nothing more than a defense mechanism for surviving the mean streets of Southeast DC. As he began to do better in school, she saw the change in his attitude and demeanor that were a direct result of his newfound confidence and support   system.

She made a mental note to follow-up and say thank you to Dean Johnson because she was sure his stern talks with Justin helped motivate the teenager as well.

"It was no problem at all. I'm glad I could help," she replied. "And like I always say, someone did those things for me."

Alonna gently returned her smile and squeezed Melody's hand.

"So, how are things going here?"

"Really good," answered Melody.

"April called out today because her daughter was sick, but we found a substitute for her group. Victor called and said that that all is going well with the planning for the conference, but he left a voice message on your direct line."

April and Victor were part of her new staff, and Alonna knew that the new grant would allow them to move from part-time workers to full-time staff for the season. She could not wait to share the news with them.

"Also, I almost forgot," Melody added as she handed Alonna a certified letter. "The Governor's office called today to follow up with that letter in your hand." Before Alonna could open the letter, Melody had made her around the table and gave Alonna a congratulatory hug.

"Congratulations lady, you were nominated for the Young Woman Humanitarian Award!"

Alonna was in disbelief. She opened the letter and scanned through it. She would have to do a mini-investigation later to find out who nominated her for this award. She tried her best to match Melody's excitement, and resolved that in that department, Melody would beat her any day. If this nomination was serious, this was probably the biggest accolade she'd ever received. The Young Woman Humanitarian Award was usually awarded to up and coming philanthropists and movers and shakers in the DC area, not ordinary people like her.

"Thank you so much, Melody. This is a huge honor." Alonna said, still in shock.

"Thanks for all you do every day. I don't know how this place would run without you." Alonna added as she walked away.

"Sure thing," she heard Melody respond as she started walking toward her office. She was almost done packing her things, and she'd dedicated today as her final day to pack up the last of her things for the new building.

"Ms. Alonna, Ms. Alonna!"

Perhaps today was not the day for packing after all, she chuckled to herself. Alonna turned around to see Renee

158

running carefully toward her. She was five months pregnant, and Renee's belly was beginning to poke out of her petite frame. It had done her heart well when she received the telephone call from Renee that she decided to keep the baby. Alonna had spent countless nights praying that God would lead Renee to a good decision. Those prayers were answered when Alonna witnessed the miracle of her mother's change of heart.

In the last month, not only was Renee maturing as a person, but she and Alonna were also developing a deeper bond. She'd quickly learned that as independent as Renee always claimed to be, the young girl used every opportunity to hang around her. Renee reminded Alonna of her teenage self, so she always welcomed her.

"Whoa Renee, slow down! Where is the fire? How come you're not in your life skills class?" The questions came quickly.

Alonna suspected that sometimes Renee forgot she was pregnant, because she still carried on like all the other teenage girls in the group. Renee began crying. She had revealed to Alonna that the pregnancy hormones often overwhelmed her, and Alonna had come to expect the seemingly random outbursts.

"What's wrong? Come, let's go in my office." She put her hand on the small of her back to guide her in.

"No, these are happy tears," Renee replied, holding her hand up to stop Alonna. She hugged Alonna tighter than she had ever done before.

"Whew, ok, so share the good news already," Alonna replied relieved. She took the girl by her hand and led her into her office anyway.

Renee sat down in the empty chair. Alonna placed the boxes that were on her desk, to create room for herself to sit.

With tears still running down her face, Renee exclaimed, "I got into college Ms. Alonna. Howard accepted me."

Almost instantly, Alonna, too, began crying. She around the desk to hug the girl.

"Congratulations, sweetie. I am so excited for you. You worked very hard for this."

"They really want me, Ms. Alonna. I have an opportunity to make something good of myself now."

Alonna reached for a tissue and handed it to Renee.

"Yes, you do Renee," Alonna stated, "and you're going to do a great job!"

"I'm so excited, but I'm so nervous," Renee took the tissue and blotted her eyes. "No one in my family has ever been to college before, much less after having a baby." Renee said. She explained that she chose to defer her enrollment until the Spring so that she can have the baby and work out arrangements with her mother for childcare.

Alonna said a silent prayer of thanks. No many girls her age were getting the support or opportunity that Renee was getting. While the issue of teenage pregnancy was still a very serious one, she was glad to see that the Renee had accepted her situation and was determined to make the best of it.

"Well, then I guess God chose you as the perfect candidate for the job. Didn't he?"

Renee returned Alonna's smile, which was quickly followed by a look of skepticism.

"What if I don't do well? What if the work is too hard? What if I don't get enough money to pay for it? What if I have to drop out to take care of the baby?" It was Renee's turn to ask the questions.

Alonna marveled at how much Renee reminded her of herself. She had had similar questions run through her mind some years ago.

"Don't worry, you will do fine. Like we always do, we will figure out how to best support you with the baby, and if anything comes up, I have my people at Howard who will be watching you like a hawk," Alonna joked.

Renee laughed, "I believe you when you say that, Ms. Alonna. I'm going to go back to small group, but I could not wait until after class to tell you my good news." Renee reached out and gave Alonna another hug.

"Thank you," Alonna stated, "you made my day. Come by my office after class and we can talk some more. Congratulations again, future Bison."

Despite all it took to get to this point, Alonna took joy in the fact that Renee would also be a product of her alma mater. She silently said a prayer that Justin and Renee would be the first of many of her inaugural group, both locally and internationally, that would be driven enough to become pioneers in their families and role models for their peers.

Chapter 23

Things were quickly picking up for The Journey House. Six out of the nine graduating seniors in the small groups had been accepted to local colleges, and Alonna was missing Shawn less and less. She was not sure why she did it, but, strictly out of boredom, she'd accepted Nicole's request to set her up on a blind date. After seven months of separation, she no longer believed that her relationship with Shawn could be reconciled, and had agreed to go on the date.

The night of the date arrived sooner than Alonna had planned, and so far things were going very well. As she sat across from Jeff, Nicole's friend from church, she commented on how beautiful the restaurant was. From an earlier conversation, he'd taken note of her preference for Thai food and made reservations at one of the most exclusive restaurants in the area.

To most other women, Jeff would be a good catch. He was gainfully employed as an Accounts Manager for one of the top financial consulting companies in the area, he was a frequent attendee at Bethel United Methodist Church, and he was no slacker in the looks department. His broad shoulders, and bulging biceps were outlined perfectly in the baby blue sweater he wore, and his skin was the color of a Hersey's chocolate bar—just the way she liked it.

Alonna could not put her finger on it, but something was wrong. The fact remained that no matter how much she tried, no one measured up to Shawn. Despite her desperate efforts to push thoughts of him aside, she had created an unattainable standard when she met Shawn, and even though they hadn't spoken in several months she still felt like she was being unfaithful.

When Nicole first mentioned Jeff, she was surprised. In the year and a half since she started going to Redemption Nondenominational, she had never seen him with a woman. She often wondered how a good-looking, charming, and intelligent man like him was single, especially with all the women in the church. According to Nicole, Jeff had chosen to remain single while he worked on developing his relationship with God. Initially the idea sounded extreme to Alonna, but she'd grown to appreciate that sometimes it's best to tune out all other distractions while nurturing the most important relationship there would ever be.

"So, how do you like the food?" Jeff interrupted her thoughts.

"It is delicious. Thank you so much for going through the trouble of making the reservations. I know it must have been hard trying to get in here." Alonna smiled coyly.

Jeff smiled a sheepish grin and replied, "not really. The manager is a good friend of mine from high school."

Alonna laughed, "of course he is. Is there anyone in DC that you and Nicole don't know?" She was learning quickly and was quite impressed by how well connected Jeff was. Over the course of dinner, several people stopped by to say hello to him. She wondered how often he came to the restaurant.

"Of course there is," he laughed.

Their conversation at dinner remained polite, but the spark she had on her first date with Shawn was missing.

They remained cordial, and continued the conversation on the walk back to her car. Alonna gave Jeff a polite hug, and then stepped into the car. He shut the door behind her and waved adoringly as she drove away. With the exception of his stale sense of humor—compared to Shawn—Jeff was probably everything that she should be interested in, she thought to herself. He was god-fearing, handsome, accomplished, mature, well-connected, and outgoing—everything that everyone thinks is good for her. However, for some reason, her heart would not let her commit to trying out a possible relationship with him, much less a second date. She wondered to herself what was wrong with her. There were many women who would have killed to get a chance with Jeff, and here she was not the least bit interested.

She thought she might have been crazy, but it seemed a voice was cautioning her to detach now. One of the most difficult things to get over was her attachment to all of the men that she had been involved with. She'd heard this familiar voice when she met Ray, but he, too, was everything that she was suppose to like.

There were times when she wondered what her life would be like had she not allowed herself to get so attached to Shawn. She could hear the voice reasoning with her that while she could not do anything about her attachment to Shawn, she did not have to repeat the same lessons with Jeff. Alonna remained deep in thought as she drove home. She was thankful that the dark night would prevent anyone in a neighboring car from seeing that she was literally carrying on a conversation with herself. She had been

164

through heartache in the past, but this one was persistent. She had tried to shake the feelings, but it seemed she just could not keep Shawn Williams out of her thoughts and heart for an extended period of time.

Alonna's thoughts were interrupted as she heard her favorite song by Ledell, "Trusting Always." The song had taken her through many sleepless nights, as Ledell's melodic voice sang about God's goodness and mercies, and how He rewards faith. Almost suddenly Alonna felt a calm she had not felt in some time. She remember the words of her mother, as she would often quote her favorite scripture that the prayer of a righteous man is powerful and effective. She prayed a prayer for Shawn, that wherever he was, God would draw him closer to truth, and that God would grant him favor and restore his faith.

****

The dreams were occurring more frequently. This time, she'd only managed to sleep for two hours before she was awoken abruptly. Alonna dreamt that was she in a room full of teenagers who were carrying on with their usual activities, waiting for a youth outreach to begin. In the dream, Pastor Paul announced that the speaker for the evening would not be able to make it. He then called on Alonna to be the back-up speaker for the night. Alonna saw herself in the dream as she began to talk about I Kings chapter 13, and then she woke up.

Alonna had never been a biblical scholar, nor did she aspire to be. While she was often impressed by those who could regurgitate scripture and cite their references, she never felt compelled to memorize scripture to that extent. She knew the Word, and the Holy Spirit was

165

consistent in bringing relevant scriptures to her mind whenever she needed them. Naturally, because of her indifference to memorizing scripture, when she woke up she had not the slightest clue as to what 1 Kings 13 said. Alonna decided to use the scripture as her focus for the morning's devotional. Ever since she moved back, she found herself wanting to make times for the things she used to, before her life became as chaotic as it did. Through these brief encounters with God, Alonna found that she received nuggets, as Pastor Paul, called them to carry throughout her day, and to reference when things became challenging.

Although the dream was short, something in her spirit told her that the dream held some spiritual significance. As she got out of bed to grab her bible on the nightstand, Alonna thought about Shawn. Although her thoughts were no longer consumed with him, she still missed him. Remembering one of her favorite verses, she decided to take the thought captive in order to focus on spending some time with God.

Alonna walked to her new home office—the area she'd also deemed her prayer closet. Sometimes she danced in the little room, and other times she sat at the sturdy oak desk and recorded journal entries. These moments never ceased to amaze her, and she was confident that she would always leave feeling refreshed and confident to face the day. Alonna knew today would not be any different.

An hour later, Alonna sat with her head down, discontent with what she think she heard from her heavenly father during her devotional time. The scripture had been about a young man who had been misled by an old prophet. At the end, though he had good intentions of following the supposed wise counsel of the prophet, he was killed because of his disobedience of God.

Surely she'd heard wrong, and the scripture was not about obeying God even when godly people tell you things that are contradictory to what you hear from Him. Surely, there was no injustice in following wise counsel. All of her foundational understanding of God had been based on the idea that those who were older in the faith always knew better. Alonna wept as the weight of her decisions came down on her. It had been so long since she allowed the voice of God to lead her, instead of other people. She'd gotten so used to listening to other people in place of God, that she had not realized that supposed wise counsel had replaced the voice of God Himself.

Alonna thought about the repercussions of the young prophet in 1 Kings 13. He was killed by a Lion, of all things, because he disregarded what the father told him, in favor of what a prophet told him. Alonna wondered if the familiarity of the messenger, or his respectable position played a role in the young prophet's disobedience. She was certain that it came with good intentions. However, it was still disobedience.

Alonna wept in repentance. She thought back to the still small voice that had echoed to her months back that the relationship would be a story of redemption. Alonna wept. She knew that grace meant that she may not be mauled by a lion for her disobedience, but she still would not want to risk the consequence of disobedience. As she continued to cry out before God, she heard the still small voice: *let patience have its perfect work.*

Whatever was going to happen next, she knew would be a miracle from God Himself.

Chapter 24

Alonna was awestruck, which was a rare occurrence. She'd never been in the midst of so many dignitaries before, and it humbled her to think that they were all gathered together in small part to honor her. When she first learned that she was selected as the finalist for the Young Woman Humanitarian award, she thought at best she would have a picture and a short write-up in the local paper. She never expected that she would be in the room with senators, ambassadors, diplomats, and even former first ladies who would also be awarded for their humanitarian work. The bright shining light in her face, and the adulation of those she looked at in the audience from her place at the high table reminded her to keep her composure. She never got a chance to find out who nominated her, and right now, that was probably of no importance.

It seemed lately all she did was cry. Albeit tears of joy, she decided this may not be the most appropriate place to display such emotion. She silently meditated on Proverbs 18:16. Never in her wildest dreams would she have imagined that she would be in such a position for her work with The Journey House.

As she shook her last hand of the evening, Alonna thought about how she could not wait to take off the four inch heels she was wearing. If she had her own way, she would wear jeans and converse sneakers everyday and to every occasion. While she'd secretly enjoyed getting dolled up, and receiving celebrity-style treatment, all she could think about was the comfort of her bed to make up for the last few days of sleep deprivation.

She'd met the former first lady of Senegal, the Ambassador to France, and Ellen Johnson—one of the remaining living legends from the civil rights era. She'd interviewed with numerous news outlets, and relished in the fact that what they thought was a nice inspirational story, was really a testament of God's grace in her life. She was not sure if they would understand the reference, but she'd tried her best to explain that her life and The Journey House was really a transformation of beauty from ashes.

As she prepared to make her way out of the back door, Alonna heard a familiar voice call out her name. She was not sure what he was doing there, and how she had missed him the whole evening, but as she looked up their eyes locked. Besides the comfort of her bed, at that very moment, she missed him also. Their relationship was ordinary, and their aspirations simple, but they understood each other. All night she'd dodged salacious men who appeared only interested in her to meet their insatiable desire, or to have her as the completion of their trophy lives. Admittedly, while some were remarkable, none of what they had to offer had impressed her. They all paled in comparison.

She'd attended the event by herself, despite being given an extra ticket, and she assumed that some of them thought that was an indication she was single. She'd thought about inviting Jeff, but she didn't want to prolong the inevitable. For as long as her feelings were unsettled, it wouldn't be fair to him. Her only other options were Ari and Nicole, and both traveled out of town for work.

It was only when Shawn walked up to her that Alonna realized that she had not stopped staring at him since she turned around.

"What are you doing here?"

It was their first conversation in some time, and she could not think of anything else to ask him.

"Congratulations." He flashed his famous smile. "You look amazing." He glanced over the form-fitting black dress that Alonna was wearing.

She had to admit herself, that she was looking very good that night. Her usually loose curls were pinned up, and she'd gotten her makeup professionally done just for the event.

"Thanks," she cracked a laugh. "So, what are you doing here?"

"My professor had an extra ticket and invited me."

"Oh, that was nice of her."

"He thought I could use some inspiration for my research." Alonna smiled to herself. She could never put anything past him.

"Well, that was nice of him. You look good too by the way."

He did. Only once had Alonna seen him in a suit, and he'd looked amazing then. Now, he looked even better in the dark suit and the light blue tie that seemed to bring out his eyes. She didn't think it was possible, but he seemed even more handsome now than he did the last time she saw him.

Shawn smiled back. "Anyway, I'm not going to hold you much." He reached over to hug her. "I just wanted to say congratulations. I am glad you are finally getting the recognition you deserve." Alonna thought she saw a hint of sadness in his eyes.

"I appreciate that. I hope you are doing well." She wished she could think of more creative ways to extend their conversation, but her mind was drawing a blank.

Their embrace was awkward, but it was also one of the most comfortable places that Alonna had been in some time. As she walked back to her car, she said another silent prayer for Shawn. She could only hope that the seeds that had been planted would grow and that God would restore his faith, if not for their relationship, so he could be in right standing with Him.

If The Journey House had taught her nothing else so far, it was about how fleeting life could be. She'd heard the horror stories of kids whose friends died from violence, and young girls whose innocence was lost because of reckless decisions. Everyday she was reminded that life is not guaranteed. She could only hope that Shawn would have an experience that would lead him to understand the same.

Chapter 25

As usual, Pastor Paul had delivered a rousing sermon. Alonna thought about how ironic it was that today's message was about the value of relationships. He had spoken passionately about how God values relationship, so much so that He sent His own son so that everyone would be able to have a relationship with Him. Pastor Paul referenced several scriptures to highlight man's humanity and tendency to disappoint, but explained that God is the only one who can never disappoint people. In light of her recent conversation with her father, the message struck a cord with Alonna. By the looks of other congregants, it seemed the message hit home for many of them as well.

As Pastor Paul continued the altar call for the day, Alonna quietly agreed in prayer as he interceded on behalf of the nonbelievers in the congregation that morning. As had become her habit, she said a prayer for Shawn. She prayed that wherever he was, the Holy Spirit would convict him, comfort him, and truly show him God's love.

Alonna remembered when she rededicated her life to the Lord. It was not because of the sermon, or a powerful prayer. She had simply come to the realization that she was inadequate and unreliable by herself. No matter how hard she tried to love people, she always failed at loving at least two people, namely her father and Ray, unconditionally. No matter how much she tried to forgive Ray, the thought of what he put her through would cause her heart to race and she would begin to entertain thoughts of vengeance.

She'd grown up in the church. She knew of the message of Christ dying on the cross for her. She still thought about her youth pastor, who, one time told her that the message of the gospel was as simple as God Himself wanting to walk with Alonna and exchange her burdens for His. From what she'd understood that day, He had none. It seemed an unfair exchange, but she was desperate to give hers up. She was tired of being tired. The day Alonna realized that, she said a prayer in her bedroom. She explained to something unknown at the time how desperate she was for someone to heal her and to clean her of the terrible mistakes she'd made. Since she cried out, her life had never been the same.

As Alonna thought about that night, she continued her prayer for Shawn. She prayed that God would miraculously touch his heart. As she said her own prayers, she could also hear Pastor Paul's in the background. His prayer always seemed to be a sermon in itself. Alonna enjoyed how he thoroughly and carefully laid out his requests before God.

As Pastor Paul began to pray louder, Alonna slid to her knees and fervently joined the pastor in praying for those in the congregation and the absent loved ones who had yet to exchange their burdens for God's. Before she knew it, she was sobbing as she cried out to God for Shawn and her father. She prayed that the same God who had been with her and never forsook her during the most trying times of her life, would also avail Himself to two of the most important people in her life.

Minutes seemed to go by before Alonna felt the soft touch on her back. With tears in her eyes, Alonna looked up to see Nicole, who also appeared to be in tears. She immediately sat up, back to her seat. Alonna followed Nicole's eyes to see what she was looking at. She blinked her eyes to make sure that she was seeing correctly.

Walking to the front of the church was Shawn. He walked with his usual confidence, but Alonna could see the humility as he also walked with his head slightly bowed. Immediately, Alonna lifted her hands—the only response she knew to have, in awe of her Father's ability to answer prayers. She'd had no idea that Shawn was in the building that day.

Alonna stood up and could hardly control herself. This time, her tears were not tears of sadness, but of joy. She resisted the urge to run to the front with him and put her arms around him. She could hear the spirit affirming her and telling her that this had to be a personal decision for Shawn.

A string of praises fell from Alonna's mouth. She thanked God for hearing her prayers. She thanked Him for saving Shawn. She thanked God for the freedom that she knew he was about to experience. She'd resolved weeks earlier, that even if she and Shawn did not reconcile, she would make his salvation a consistent praying point. She looked over at Nicole, who was also in prayer. She had no words sufficient to thank God for answering prayers. She grew up listening to her mother's testimonies, and for the first time in a long time, she was experiencing one herself.

Alonna listened as Pastor Paul spoke into his microphone.

"Saints, we praise God. The bible says that even the

angels rejoice at one who repents and comes into the kingdom."

Alonna could hear the string of amens and hallelujahs.

"Saints," Pastor Paul continued, "we need to join the angels and thank God for our new brother in Christ today."

Alonna knew Shawn very well, and she smirked as she noticed how uncomfortable he appeared with the attention he was getting. She said a silent prayer that God would send a godly man that would walk with him in truth and for accountability.

Pastor Paul continued, "Brethren, join me in prayer for God's beloved."

Alonna stood up along with the rest of the congregation.

"Father, daddy, Yahweh, we thank you for your son," Pastor Paul said into the microphone.

"Amen," the congregants responded as if on cue.

"We thank you that you saw fit to mark today as the day that he would realize how much you love him." He said as he placed his hand on Shawn's shoulder. "Father you called Peter blessed because he recognized that Heaven revealed Christ's identity to him, and not flesh and blood. Father we thank you that flesh and blood have not revealed your identity to this brother, but that heaven has."

Alonna could hear the older ladies in the back with their shouts of "hallelujah."

"Father, we pray that as flesh did not reveal it, flesh would not take it away. We pray that from this day on, this dear brother would yearn for you. I pray that you would continue revealing yourself to him. Father gird him up in

175

your truth, and keep life's storms from snatching what you have planted in him."

Pastor Paul continued to pray for Shawn. He prayed that Shawn would not experience guilt from previous mistakes, but that his joy would be renewed and that he would feel compelled to share testimonies of his transformation with others. Pastor Paul also prayed that Shawn would spend the rest of his days living out and being known as a mighty man of God. Alonna whole heartedly agreed with that prayer. She opened her eyes and caught a glimpse of Shawn, who now also appeared to be in tears.

In the time that she had known him, she could count on one finger how many times she had seen him crying. She knew well that this was the only emotional response anyone could have for what he was experiencing. So many others, including herself, had experienced the same feeling and transformation.

Those who were not standing before, were now on their feet clapping as Shawn was escorted to the back by a deacon. Alonna kept her head down. She did not want to make eye contact, or do anything that would distract him from the experience he'd just had. She felt the peace of God come over her that there would be plenty of time for talking later, but this moment was simply about him and His God.

Epilogue

Six Months later

Nicole and Ari could not believe it. They looked over at Alonna, who was wearing the same violet dress she had on the day she met Shawn. Despite their efforts to talk her out of it, and into Nicole's Vera Wang dress that she could now fit, Alonna had insisted that she and Shawn wanted to wear the same clothes because it was significant to them. Neither of them understood it, but it was Alonna's day, so they left well enough alone. They were unsure of what the future held, but both were certain that Shawn and Alonna's marriage would be one for the books because they loved each other without hesitation or bounds.

Alonna was all smiles. This was not the way she or her girlfriends had planned any of their weddings when they used to stay up for hours and talk about their futures, but her willingness to make things right before God far outweighed her fantasies. She and Shawn and already discussed their plans to continue with the civil wedding now, to be followed next spring by a celebration of their vows with their closest friends and family members. When she first had the idea, Alonna had originally anticipated thirty guests, but before she knew it, there were over 200 people on their guest list. Thankful for Nicole's knack for administrative work and organizational skills, the planning of the couple's celebration was coming along quite well.

In a matter of months so much had changed for them. Alonna thought back to when she was sixteen years old. She'd made a list of every quality she'd wanted in a future husband. At the time, the idea was just for kicks, but over the years she'd changed it several times it to reflect her growth and maturity. In recent years, it was supposed to serve as a guideline for her dating relationships. The number one thing, of course, should have been that the man is a man of God. While he did not initially possess the first quality, Shawn consistently proved himself faithful with the others. He was caring, funny and loving, but none of that mattered as much. Alonna thought about how incredible it was to witness that with Shawn's renewed faith, she was also seeing maturity in many other areas that she'd listed. She'd learned a valuable lesson about the peace that comes with not settling.

Today, along with her family and their four closest friends—Nicole, Ari, Mike and Chris, the two stood in front of the judge. They had prepared for this during the numerous hours of premarital counseling, but still Alonna could not settle the butterflies in her stomach.

She looked over at Nicole and Mike. Never in her wildest imaginations would she have thought that the two would end up together. Life had a funny way of bringing things and people together. Alonna smiled because she knew that despite the fact that it took them so long, her best friend and cousin were both in good hands with each other. Since they got together, Alonna had never seen Nicole happier. Most importantly, Nicole was happy to report that her mother was finally off her back.

"Ms. Jones and Mr. Williams, is this everyone you want present for this ceremony?" The judge interrupted her thoughts.

"Yes," they both answered in unison.

"Alright, well let's proceed," Judge Saunders said with a smile on his face.

Alonna could not believe that her friend from Howard was now a judge in the state of Virginia. At age 32, Kevin Saunders was the youngest judge in Arlington County. She remembered the study groups that they were in together, and how they'd talk about their plans for the future. He was very much living his, and while Alonna's plans did not quite work out the way she'd envisioned, she was living beyond her wildest imagination. Alonna smiled back at her friend.

She could hear Shawn clear his throat and she knew instantly what he was thinking about—the hours that would follow the ceremony—hours that he'd been counting down to for what seemed like an eternity. Alonna gave him a playful jab.

"Alright Mr. Williams, I get it," Kevin joked. "Let's begin, shall we?"

As Kevin read the vows, Alonna willingly repeated after him—promising to love and respect her soon-to-be husband till death did them apart. When it came time for Shawn's turn, Judge Saunders said, "I understand you wrote something that you want to say."

"Yes sir," Shawn responded.

Judge Saunders extended his hand in a gesture to give Shawn the floor.

Shawn nervously took out a piece of paper from his back pocket. His hands seemed to tremble as he unfolded

179

the paper. Alonna gently touched his arm as a show of support.

"Baby," Shawn began, "I mean Alonna."

She smiled back at him. She knew how uncomfortable he was, and hoped that her smile offered him the support he needed.

"I decided to write my vows to you because I want you to know, in my own words, how much you mean to me."

Alonna nodded, and she started to feel the tears welling up in her eyes. Shawn had never been one for many words or such public display of affection.

"Since the day that I met you, my life has never been the same. You have managed to challenge all my ideas about what I wanted and thought I needed in life."

Alonna looked over at Mike and Chris who were smirking. They were Shawn's closest friends, and they knew about all of his boyhood philosophies. One of which she recently learned included staying a bachelor until he was fifty, and then settling down with a twenty-five year old. She'd given him a piece of her mind when she heard that.

Shawn ignored his friends' antics and continued.

"Alonna, I love you so much. You brighten up my day with your smile. Your strength and dependence on our God is inspiring and pushes me to be a better man. Not a day goes by that I don't thank God for bringing you into my life. Had I not met you, I shudder to think about what my life would be like."

Shawn reached over to wipe the tears that were now flowing down Alonna's cheeks.

"Alonna, I love you," he continued although his own voice was now full of emotion.

"For as long as you'll let me, I want to be there for you. I want to be there through thick and thin. I want to grow old with you. I want to protect you and I promise to always lead you, as your husband, toward all things pure, righteous, and wonderful."

Had she not witnessed his transformation herself, she would have struggled to believe that this was the same guy she met over a year ago. His desires were the first things she'd noticed had changed since he decided to recommit his life to God. She knew that to hear him say such things was truly a miraculous work from God.

Alonna, now unable to control herself, reached across and hugged him.

Their friends broke up in applause—Alonna could hear Nicole and Ari sniveling in the back.

Kevin cleared his throat in an effort to break up the couple's embrace.

"So, I take it that this means you take Alonna to be your wife?" he joked.

"Yes sir," Shawn said assuredly, his gaze not leaving   Alonna's.

"Well alright now. You may kiss your bride."

Alonna could hear their friends cheering and whistling in the background. None of that mattered to her. All that mattered was that, in the eyes of God, they were one and they were right. She was now the proud Mrs. Alonna Williams.

Alonna allowed herself to relax in her husband's embrace as she hid her head in his chest. She said a prayer of thanks to her heavenly father for bestowing such a wonderful gift to her.

****

An hour later, the couple sat with their friends and family at Sala Thai. Neither wanted anything elaborate, just a small luncheon to celebrate their union. As she sat across from Shawn, Alonna still found it difficult to believe how God had redeemed the entire situation. Her mother immediately fell in love with Shawn, upon hearing his story and observing how deeply Shawn cared for her. Her father on the other hand, had given her a hard time initially. It was Shawn who won him over by agreeing to work on his classic car.

His parents, however, were a different story. Shawn had given them very little information regarding their relationship. In fact, she would not have been surprised if neither knew about their wedding. Regardless of the struggles he still faced, if she could write her life's novel herself, she could have not drafted a better lead. In Shawn, she'd found an earthly demonstration of the Father's grace. He willingly and freely accepted her life story and vowed to protect her through what she knew were bound to be some tough times ahead. A year ago she questioned everything. Now, she marveled at how far they'd come.

Pulling her out of her trance, Shawn reached for her hand across the table. "You know I love you right?"

Alonna smiled, "barely a day has gone by that you have not reminded me."

"Good," he stated, "I never expected to meet and fall in love with someone like you."

Alonna looked at him daringly, "what do you mean by someone like me, Mr. Williams?"

"As soon as I said that, I realized I'd set myself up," he laughed out loud. "I mean someone who is so patient and kind, Mrs. Williams."

Alonna thought back to the day they met. At the time, she'd only encouraged the relationship with him because she was unemployed, bored, and lonely. She'd expected what had become the norm for her—guys who would entertain her for some time, only for the relationship to go sour for one reason or another. However, she soon realized that her feelings for him were different from the others. When she began to see how the Lord was working on both of their hearts and lives, she could no longer hide or suppress her feelings.

She recalled how she'd been confused and embarrassed about their relationship. Now he was the confident leader that she'd needed him to be all along. Instead of begging him to go to church on Sundays, he'd become so involved that Pastor Paul asked him to co-lead the youth ministry with one of the elders in the church. She marveled at the fact that God had indeed put together a lovely thing.

"So, what do you think?" he asked.

Alonna snapped out of her thoughts apologetic, "I'm sorry sweetheart, what did you say?" she asked.

"Baby, is everything ok?" he asked. He was always very concerned about her. She thanked God for that. There was nothing like having been with someone who did not care, to make you appreciate someone who did.

"Yes, I'm sorry. I just didn't hear what you said."

"I was saying that we should spend thanksgiving with your parents, and Christmas with my dad this year," Shawn stated. "What do you think?"

Alonna nodded approvingly.

"I was thinking that it's about time that my father and I talked. Since I will have more days off during

Christmas, I will give me more time to catch up with him. That's assuming he wants to talk to me of course."

"Of course he will, honey," she squeezed his hand, "He's your dad and I'm sure he loves you very much."

Alonna smiled. God had once again shown Himself faithful in their lives. She'd spent months in prayer for her husband and his father's relationship. She knew that her husband could be stubborn. She was still in prayer that God would soften that characteristic as well, but for now she was content that there would be reconciliation this Christmas. Across the table, Alonna reached for her husband, "let's go home, Mr. Williams" she said.

"Well alright, Mrs. Williams" was all Shawn could muster as he laughed and took out fifty dollars from his wallet, enough to cover their appetizers and a tip for the waitress. He knew exactly what her catch phrase "let's go home" meant. They waved good-bye to their friends, as they walked hand in hand, thanking God for the redemption in their lives and for each other.

QUESTIONS FOR DISCUSSION

1. Alonna has had a troubled relationship with her father since her teenage years. Do you think that Alonna's relationship with her father has anything to do with her low expectations of men? How do readers know that she has low expectations of men?

2. Alonna recalls that her mother warned her about being in relationships that are unequally yoked. Would her relationship with Shawn fall into this category despite the fact that Shawn grew up in the church?

3. After their first date, Alonna suggested that Shawn go to church with her if he wanted to continue seeing her. After going to church with her for months, Shawn tells Alonna that he does not want to be her project. What did he mean by that? Was Alonna wrong to give him an ultimatum about going to church?

4. Alonna falls after three years of celibacy. How is God's grace shown in her situation? What could, if anything, she have done to prevent it from happening? She recalls that her mother used to tell her she was too hard on herself. Does Alonna have reason to be in this area?

5. Why do you think Alonna kept her secret for so long? Should she have chosen Shawn to be the first one she revealed her secret to?

6. In Chapter 15, Alonna wakes up from a dream about rotten teeth. Despite the fact that the dream scares her and she begins to see herself with a tarnished image, she says

that it is the first time in three years that she'd received so much peace. Is it possible for someone to be afraid and at peace at the same time? In what way does this dream come true later in the novel?

7. Renee's name means second chance? In what ways does Renee symbolize a second chance for Alonna?

8. Alonna decided that if her father did not want to extend the olive branch, she would. During their conversation, he asks her why it took her so long to come back home. What can readers assume from her response about what home is? Based on this definition, are there other characters in this novel that you would say found their way home?

CPSIA information can be obtained at www.ICGtesting.com
Printed in the USA
LVOW09s2136110215

426712LV00010B/153/P